THE *Vengeful* QUEEN

THE HALE MAFIA BOOK II

B L M U T E

EDITING: One Love Editing

COVER DESIGNER AND FORMATTING: TRC Designs

THE *Vengeful* QUEEN

THE HALE MAFIA BOOK II

B L M U T E

PLAYLIST

Wait for Me- Raphael Lake, Ben Fisher

You should be sad- Halsey

I Know What You Did Last Summer- Shawn Mendes, Camila Cabello

I'm Not Angry Anymore- Warwick Smith

Shutter Island- Jessie Reyez

Needed Me- Rihanna

You broke me first- Tate McRae

Pills N Potions- Nicki Minaj

Ghost- Halsey

You should see me in a crown- Billie Eilish

"Vengeance is in my heart, death in my hand, blood and revenge are hammering in my head." – William Shakespeare

CHAPTER ONE

Charlie

The lights of the room are dim and my vision is foggy. Something or someone is there. As I move closer, the silhouette before me flickers like the reel of an old movie. I try to process who or what is standing before me. Suddenly, I'm met with a touch. It's a familiar feel. His hand twitches on my cheek, and my thoughts race. The touch of his strong hand kindles memories of passion, but is this real?

I move my palm over his and press it harder into my face, willing myself to believe I'm not crazy. "Teddy?" I question on a whisper. My voice is shaky and weakens with the sound of his name.

"My beautiful Monkshood. I've missed you."

I almost melt at his words. A voice so raspy, so deep. A

voice I've missed so much. I let myself soften in his loose hold for a moment before reality, the reality I've been living, comes crashing back.

"You're dead," I state, stepping away. His movements mimic mine as he follows me back down the steps. One stride after the other, his steps imitate my pattern, almost stepping on my toes, until my back is met with resistance. I turn to see Lucas standing behind me.

I can hardly face him. His appearance is somewhat solemn. His head hangs low, and his once balled fists now fall to his sides loosely.

"You lied to me," I fume. My sense of disbelief quickly gives way to anger.

He doesn't try to argue or explain his actions to me. He knows he's been caught, and there is no point.

"Why?" I croak out. It's a question to both Teddy and Lucas. Technically, they both lied to me.

"I did what had to be done," Teddy says coolly, feeding me the same line he has a million times before. Lucas, on the other hand, doesn't speak. He continues to appear defeated and portrays somewhat of an emotional indifference.

Although Teddy's answer irritates me, Lucas's silence cuts deeper, leaving an exposed wound. After everything he and I have been through, I expected more from him.

I raise my hand and ball my fist before sending it flying into his nose. His body sags slightly to the side after the impact, his head staying dipped low.

"You fucking lied to me!" A scream from deep within forces its way from my mouth.

A dark chuckle bubbles from his throat as he stands back straight. Blood drips from his nose, down to his chest, coating the thin gold chain around his neck and his crisp white button-down.

He wipes his nose with the back of his hand roughly before tilting his head back, looking at me down the bridge of his nose. "Julius knew too. And Carl. And *him*." He points behind me, no doubt, to Teddy.

"I reported back to him with how you were doing, how you were running things. He knew you were a mess too!" he yells, shaking the bones inside my body with something that can only be described as fear.

I've never heard Lucas lash out. Sure, I've seen him mad, but I've never seen him like *this*. His body is twitching, his eyes are dark, and his chest is heaving a mile a minute, but it doesn't stop me. It only fuels me to continue.

"The difference between you and them"—I jab my finger over my shoulder, pointing at Julius by the door, Carl lingering to the side of the steps, and Teddy right behind me—"is that I had more trust in you. Julius doesn't talk. Carl seems like he couldn't give a fuck less, and Teddy was dead for all I knew! You're the one I trusted the most. You're the one—" I cut myself off before I can spill the words.

"I'm what?" Lucas presses, tilting his head to the side with a grin and wicked gleam in his eyes.

"Fuck you," I whisper, shoving his body away from mine.

When I turn back around, I'm met with Teddy's chest. I glance up catching his eyes but quickly look away when I see the confusion swirling within. I sidestep him and stomp back up the steps, pausing in front of Julius.

He makes no attempt to stop me as I slap him across the face. I glance at Carl and see him widen his stance. I flip him the bird, then charge inside, slamming the door behind me before any of them can follow.

A lot can change in a matter of weeks. People grow, people die, and the hands of a clock never stop moving. Much the same, my life has had a staggering transition over the past four weeks.

When my dad was murdered, I thought my life couldn't get any worse. I was left alone in the world with no mother to speak of. An adult orphan.

Until Teddy.

He started out a monster, and I never expected to want his help. I never expected to see him in a new light. And I most definitely never expected to fall in love with him.

When he died, or faked his own death rather, I realized my life could get worse. The only man I had given my heart to was gone. I fell so hard and fast for Teddy even though he and I were never destined to be together. We came from different worlds, had different beliefs. Two separate trains in danger of derailing yet going a million miles a minute down a dead-end track. Complete opposites of one another but still so perfectly right together.

My being was completely crushed the night that he died. The grief came in waves, disrupting my sleep, stealing my appetite and thoughts alike. My heart had become stale. It was mutilated into a bloody, mangled organ, and to be honest, I didn't even recognize it. It didn't even beat the same way.

Until Lucas.

I sink against the bedroom door as I close it and let the memories of the last few weeks flip through my mind. The memories I've tried to suppress, to forget. I tried so hard to take away their power to prove to myself that I could move on. But they linger in the back of my mind like dusty books on a shelf. Their pages are sharp and sting like a paper cut, yet here I sit, opening their cover.

Six days after Teddy's "death," Lucas walked in on me on the bathroom floor. I was a mess. Tears flowed like a river down my face, and my heart ached so bad. I never knew how I would recover. Lucas picked me up, tipped my chin high, and told me, "*Let it all out. Scream and cry. Beat the walls, break the vases. Do whatever you need to do to feel better, but leave it in this room. You're in charge now and held at a higher standard. You can't be weak—you are the queen.*"

At first, his words pissed me off. How was I supposed to run things when I just lost my lover, let alone be expected *not* to cry. *Not* to feel. My favorite thing, it seemed, was to take my anger out on him. To use him as my own personal punching bag. So I reached up to hit him, but he caught my hand.

When his hand wrapped around mine, something clicked.

Something changed. I don't know if it was the mere touch from a man, the longing for Teddy, or the fact I was so angry I didn't know what to do. But whatever it was drove me forward. I pushed my body into him and crashed my lips to his. At first, he didn't stop. He let his tongue swirl with mine and pushed his hands through my hair. But then like someone poured a glass of cold water on him, he broke away. His whisper stung as he muttered something about not being able to do that to Teddy.

After that, I still let him hold me. I needed his touch. I needed someone to calm the shakes, someone to make the pain go away, and for some reason, Lucas was that person. We agreed to never cross that invisible line again, but we still kept our routine.

Every night he would come into my room and hold me as I sobbed, but the next morning he would leave before I woke. It was our own dirty little secret that wasn't even really that dirty, but we both knew it was wrong. Even though we never took it to the next level, never let our lips explore one another's again, it still wasn't right. Maybe somewhere deep down in my subconscious, I knew Teddy was alive.

We never spoke about our nights together. I was too ashamed of myself. As for him? I often wondered what it was for him, but he too kept our secret. No one ever knew. Just him and I. Whatever budding feelings that were starting to grow between us would be pushed away and ignored. I chalked it up to nothing more than grief, and it all seemed like a perfect plan. It all went well until I realized he and Julius were hiding something. Quiet phone calls abruptly ended when I would walk into a room. Randomly sneaking away at odd times. And the final blow… knowing Teddy was alive while I wallowed and did my best to run the shit show he left me.

Anger threatens to explode out of me, but I do my best to push it down. I start pacing the room, wearing a trail into the carpet, when the door opens and Teddy walks in.

"Monkshood?"

My eyes catch his, and suddenly all of the anger is replaced with guilt. "Why?" I question, doing my best to suppress the guilt licking at my stomach, making me feel sick, as I look down.

The question is more to me. *Why did you do it, Charlie? You're so angry with him for lying, but isn't that what you're doing?*

I shake my head, silencing my internal thoughts as I bring my eyes back to his, waiting for his answer.

He scrubs his hand down his face, then finally opens his mouth. "I did what had—"

I hold my hand up and cut him off. "Don't. I want the truth. You owe me that much."

I watch as his eyes narrow into slits like he's debating on what to tell me. "I thought if I faked my death, whoever is running the cartel would show themselves and we could finally get answers."

"Well, did they?" I ask. As angry as I am, with him and myself, I still want to find the answers to my dad's murder. I want to end whoever took him from me.

He closes the gap between us, and his hand reaches towards

my brow. His fingers grasp a strand of my hair, and he gently pushes it behind my ear. "Please just let me love you tonight. I've missed your touch." He skims his hand over my collarbone. "Your scent." He leans in and inhales next to my hair. "And your lips." Before I realize what is happening, he presses his lips to mine lightly, almost testing the waters to see what I'll do.

The electricity that's been enough to power skyscrapers still bounces between us and sets every nerve ending in my body on fire. My knees turn to putty as his tongue flicks over my own, giving me the slightest taste of him.

I want to get lost in the escape he's willing to give me, but I still have questions, and I still want answers.

I pull away from him and shoot my eyes to the floor. "I can't, Teddy."

When I raise my head again and meet his stare, I shiver. The coldness radiating from his eyes is chilling. "Have you just moved on, is that it?" he questions. "Or is it the fact I'm not Lucas?"

His words hit me somewhere deep where it hurts. I pause my reply and take a step back to study him. I'm not the only one that has changed. His changes are slight, but I can see them clear as day.

Dark stubble coats his chin and cheeks with small bits of gray peppered within sparingly. His eyes that used to burn so bright are now almost dull and lack the vivid blue I love so much. As my thoughts race, I can see he's waiting on me to speak.

"What are you talking about?" The words come out horse, almost like my mouth doesn't want to comply with my lie. It knows what I've done.

"I saw the exchange between you both. He looks at you—" He rakes his hand through his hair roughly, cutting himself off, before tugging it loose and punching the air.

"He looks at me like what, Teddy?" I step closer and circle the beast that inhabits the man I love.

"He looks at you the way I look at you, Charlie! Are you so blind you can't see it?"

Another jab to the painful spot deep down in me. "I—" I cut myself off because I'm not even sure what to say.

"But you know what's worse than that?" He steps forward, running the back of his hand along my face and down my collarbone again. "You look at him the same way."

Something in me shatters, and that deep painful place comes floating to the surface of my chest. I react on impulse and slap my hand across his face. "How dare you!" I whisper-shout, and suddenly, the beast is no longer caged.

Teddy moves quickly, stepping forward so his body is pressed against mine, and wraps his hand around my throat. He turns me around to face him and backs me against the wall. Normally it would excite me, but this time there is nothing exciting about it. My shoulder blades dig into the wall painfully as he pushes against me. His hold tightens on my throat, letting his short fingernails bite into my soft skin.

"Make no mistake of who I am, Charlotte," he says through clenched teeth. "I tried to be soft and understanding when I brought you here, and I'm afraid it's given you the wrong image of me."

His hand tightens around my neck as black spots paint my vision.

"I don't fucking share. You are *mine* and *only mine.* If I catch you with Lucas, I will kill him while you watch, then fuck you in his blood. Don't mistake my kindness for weakness, Monkshood."

He shoves me harder into the wall before releasing me and stepping away. He straightens his suit jacket, rolls his shoulders, then exits the room quietly.

I sink to the floor and hold back the screams that so desperately want to escape me. Finally, I have met the man everyone fears, and I have no doubt in my mind that he would kill me.

CHAPTER TWO

Teddy

As the door clicks closed behind me, all of my frustration detonates and the only person I want to see right now is Lucas.

His bedroom door is closed with no light shining through the crack at the bottom, so I walk to the gym. I break through the threshold and see him standing in the center shirtless, hitting the red punching back as it sways lightly.

"Enough," I shout, pulling his attention to me.

His eyes catch mine, and I can see the defeat in them. He dips his head slowly, then raises it again. "Boss." His voice is weak.

I rub my chin before unbuttoning my suit jacket and throwing it to the floor. I flip the cuffs of my sleeves, rolling them over and over until they reach my elbows. "Tell me, son, did you enjoy fucking my woman? Did her pussy feel so good that it made you forget where your loyalty lies?"

He shakes his head, then widens his stance. "I never slept with her."

The conviction in his words make me want to believe him, but I know there is still something between him and Charlie, and I need to squash it now.

"I have given you and your brother anything you could ever want or need for the past eight years, and Emil has provided several women who fall at your feet. So, why Charlotte?"

He inhales a sharp breath, then releases it. "It isn't what you think, boss."

I step closer and grip the back of his head, pulling him to my shoulder, as I whisper in his ear. "It is exactly what I think." I pull the piece from my holster and gently run the cold metal barrel alongside his temple. He flinches as my thumb teases the safety. "Consider this your warning. Next time, I won't hesitate to pull the fucking trigger."

I kiss his dark hair and push him away. I stare at him and smile, putting away the gun. I kiss my knuckles and begin driving them into his face. Over and over I hit him, and he doesn't move or try to defend himself. My fists pound into his nose, then move to his ribs until he falls and crumples to the ground.

I wipe the sweat trickling from my forehead. "We will not speak of this again. If I catch you so much as looking at *my fucking woman* again, I will kill you."

I jab my foot into his side as a parting gift, then pick up my now wrinkled suit jacket and leave the gym. Once I make it back down the hallway, I linger by Charlie's door and debate on going inside. I shake my head and continue to the front door. I know if she smarts off to me again, I'm not sure I'd be able to control myself.

I slip back into the night without another word to anyone.

CHAPTER THREE

Cameron

She knows now.

I've been watching Charlie ever since I saw her at the bank with one of the twins. I never took the time to learn who is who because they aren't important to me. They're nothing more than Theodore's attack dogs. Or were, shall I say, now that he's gone.

I don't think I've ever rejoiced more in my life than the night I heard the news, but it was short-lived. I've wanted Charlie longer than I can even think back. When Theodore died, I thought it would be the perfect time to swoop in and play the hero and comfort her while she cried, but I never got the chance. Those lowlife twins never leave her side. I wouldn't be surprised if they're fucking her at this very moment. Running their filthy hands through her long brown hair. Kissing her perfectly pale skin with their disgusting lips.

I clench my fists and push the thoughts away. It should be me there with her. It was always supposed to be me.

My thoughts race as I stare out the small round window. After what seems like an eternal flight, I can finally feel the plane beginning to descend. The only people on board are the pilot and me, yet, having all this quiet time to reflect, I can't help but feel like I have just had an entire conversation with a stranger. When I saw Charlie park in front of that storage unit, I knew it was over. I had been watching her and trying to put together my own leads. I thought I had a lucky break when I figured out her dad had a unit, but that ended abruptly once she found it first.

I'm not sure what he hid inside, but the old man was a fucking prick. I wouldn't be surprised if there was dirt on me in there. He followed me and David for too long. It's one of the reasons he was killed, and I couldn't be happier that I'm one of the people who put that motherfucker in a grave.

The scenery changes as we approach the runway. I can feel the slight bumps from the landing gear as it caresses the asphalt. I gather my things and thank the pilot as I exit the plane. The steps are narrow and steep, but I make my way to the bottom and head for the car waiting on the tarmac.

I've always maintained a low profile when it came to my dealings with the cartel, but that's all about to go out the window. Charlie is in the clutches of the mafia, my number one annoyance and enemy. I don't care about staying hidden anymore. All I care about is getting her to her rightful spot beside me.

The driver nods as I enter the car. I can hear the monotonous hiss of the tires as they begin to pound the recently rain-washed highway. The car continues to veer down curvy roads and onto beaten paths before it finally slows in front of my final destination. I step out and take in what little scenery exists. A brick walkway leads through a white picket-style fence. Just beyond that, a long and narrow two-story house with wooden-framed windows sits solemn with little decoration. I readjust the Beretta tucked in my waistband as I approach the door at the top of the steps and knock. Let's hope Sebastian is home.

The door swings open and I'm met with the man himself. The combination of his thick black mustache, stature, and baritone, raspy voice makes him a very intimidating leader. His lip curls up in disgust as he looks at me. "*Puto cerdo.*" *Fucking pig* is all he says.

I roll my eyes and stuff my hands in my pockets. "I have information. Do you want it or not?"

He tips his chin. "I don't need anything from you. I don't lay in the mud with *pigs.*"

For years I've gone round and round with Sebastian. He hates me because I'm a cop, and I hate him simply for putting my cousin in the crossfire of his shit. What he doesn't know is my badge means nothing to me. I only took the job to help David, but now he won't listen.

"You can either listen to what I have to say or find David

dead by tomorrow."

His eyes widen the slightest bit. I knew that would get his attention.

I continue. "The girl who took over Hale's territory?" He nods, urging me to go on. "She's the daughter of the man David and I took out. The one who was weaseling his way toward you."

"The old cop?"

I nod. "That's the one. And I can tell you from experience, she isn't what you think. She's probably worse than all the Hales put together. When she wants something, she doesn't stop until she has it. I've moved shit around, hiding small pieces of evidence about her dad, but I think she's finally putting it together. Of course, nothing will point to you. It'll all point to David. So, if you value his work, I suggest you keep listening."

He bites his lip and crosses his arms. "Keep going."

"I have a buddy who works for the ATF. He's willing to come down and find some hard evidence to throw the Hales away. From there, you can handle it how you want behind bars, and I'll handle the girl."

He lets out a laugh. "You expect me to depend on another pig?"

"If you want to keep David around, you will." I level my eyes with him.

"I'll think about it. Now—" He points to the car waiting at the end of his drive. "—get out of my city."

I turn and walk back to the car. I am confident Sebastian won't turn down such an offer, but then again, maybe he will. The cartel doesn't work with anyone in uniform. David associating with me is already sketchy as fuck to them, but he's proved his loyalty. He's done things no one else would do, like killing a cop. He's earned their trust. I'm only hoping I can do the same. For my cousin's sake.

Charlie won't stop until she puts all of the pieces together. I just hope I can get to her before the cartel does. Her vendetta against me just grew by the millions if her dad kept anything on me stashed away, but I'm praying she'll look past it and see the bigger picture. I did what had to be done to protect my family. It sucks she's caught in the crossfire of it, but still. I can be so much more for her. I can do so much more for her. She doesn't belong with criminals like the Hales. She belongs with me.

CHAPTER FOUR

"Where did it come from?" I throw the now opened envelope onto my desk and wait for the twins to answer.

Julius stays silent, as always, while Lucas keeps his eyes glued to the floor. His swollen cheek and bruised nose show my message was received loud and clear last night.

"I don't know. The guard from that night never reported anything suspicious. Said he never saw anything either other than Cameron, but the note was there before he showed up. That's the only lead we had." Lucas shrugs weakly.

I pull the paper from the envelope and reexamine the words. They are typed in bold black ink. The paper is thin and has many creases as if it had been folded and unfolded multiple times.

You belong with me, and I will have you. Mark my words, Charlotte.

"It's been four weeks. I expected answers by now. Go find them!" I yell.

Both Lucas and Julius stand and exit my office as Charlie walks in. She doesn't move with the same authority she used to. Instead, she walks light on her feet, almost like she's scared to make noise, and keeps her eyes on me.

"Can we talk?" she squeaks, sitting in front of me.

I nod and push the envelope and folded paper toward her. "What is this?" she asks, picking it up.

"Maybe you can tell me," I reply.

Her eyes scan the page, then shoot back to me.

"That's the envelope that was in the duffel bag the day you made that bank run and ran into Cameron."

"Lucas said it was expense reports."

I nod. "He did because he thought it was something I put in there. Instructions or something else for my 'death.'"

Her face melts the slightest bit with my words. "Who left this?"

I tell her the truth. "I don't know."

Fear replaces her expression, and suddenly all I want to do is reassure her. "I won't let anything happen to you, Monkshood. Messing with me is one thing. Messing with what belongs to me is another. It's a death sentence." The words come out harsher than expected, but I don't try to correct them.

I reach across my desk and run the back of my hand along her cheek. She flinches, then hardens under my touch. I almost feel bad. Almost. I've been too soft with her. Now it's time to let her know I don't play. It's time to show her the real man she claims to love.

I lean back in my chair and chuckle. "You can leave now." I wave my hand toward the door.

She tips her head and squints her eyes. "Who are you?"

I look behind me, then back to her while motioning to myself. "Me?" I inhale and exhale slowly. "I'm just a man questioning all he's done for a woman who clearly doesn't love him the same way."

She stands quickly with glassy eyes zeroed in on me. "That's bullshit and you know it, Teddy. I have never loved any man the way I love you. I've left all I know, broken my own moral code, all just to be with you. I look past all of the terrible shit you do *because I fucking love you*! And you know what? Sometimes I can't fucking stand it!" She throws her hands up. "Even now, right this second, I can't stand how much I love you. You're treating me like dirt, and I'm still ready to jump when you tell me."

I lick my lips and watch as her body shakes with anticipation for my next words. "Jump, then, Charlotte."

Her shoulders slouch and her head falls with a sad chuckle. "Fuck you."

I stand and circle my desk. Stopping in front of her, I grip her chin and bring her face to mine. "What was that?"

She squares her shoulders and jerks out of my grip. *There she is. The Charlie I know.*

"I said, fuck you."

A smile spreads across my face as I catch a glimpse of Lucas in the doorway out the corner of my eye. I'm not sure why he's back. I know he doesn't have answers, but what better time to show him Charlie really is mine.

"How about I just fuck you instead?" I whisper, turning her back toward the door and tucking my head into her hair.

Her body tenses again as I move to look at her. I can see the anger burning in her eyes, and the lust she can't deny.

"If you love me, show me," I say, walking my fingers down the front of her chest. "Get on your knees."

"No." She steps back and crosses her arms.

I rush to her front and grip the back of her head so she can't move. "You know you want this as bad as me. You *need* this." I grind my already hard dick into her hip.

A small moan escapes her, betraying the hard façade she's trying to keep in place.

"Come on, Monkshood. *Show me.*" I nip my teeth along her jaw.

She lets her head fall into the crook of my neck where she plants a soft kiss. I can feel the tears falling from her eyes seep through my shirt, but right now I'm not worried about her. I have something to prove.

My eyes lock with Lucas's as he watches from the doorway. He shakes his head slowly as his hands twitch by his side. He wants to stop me, to protect Charlie from the man that is me, but he won't. One thing he knows about me is I don't lie. My little tussle with him may have been a warning, but my words weren't a threat. They were a promise.

I flash him a smile before pushing Charlie to her knees. She slowly complies. I can tell she is hesitant at first, but as I stare down on her and unbuckle my belt, she ultimately submits. My eyes challenge hers. I can tell she doesn't want to do this, but she will for me. She'll always do what I ask, what I want.

I push the edge of my pants and boxers down, letting my dick spring free. Tears fall from her eyes silently as she looks to me again. *Are you sure?* She remains silent, but I can see the question in her green orbs.

I nod and tap her closed lips with the head of my length. "Show me," I hiss, and she does.

She takes me into her mouth and squeezes her eyes shut as I thrust lightly over her warm tongue, hitting the back of her throat. The tears now flow as she slobbers and gags, but I continue to facefuck her with my eyes fixed on Lucas. My head falls back, a low shrill breaking through my mouth.

"That's it," I praise her.

Lucas stands by the door unmoving, watching as I grip Charlie's long brown hair into my hands. I hold her head steady and quicken my pace, shoving my dick deeper and deeper with every thrust.

Once her gags and moans are almost deafening, he parts with a disgusted look on his face. I chuckle to myself, then explode in Charlie's mouth.

She swallows and stands. Her green eyes have a red tint with mascara painted in streaks down her face. I drag my thumb over her lips, from one side to the other, then plant a soft kiss on them.

"Good girl," I whisper, before walking out of my office, leaving her alone.

CHAPTER FIVE

Charlie

I give myself a moment to compose before I leave Teddy's office. He hasn't even been back a week, and here I am, falling to my knees to please him even though he doesn't deserve it. Maybe it's a punishment to myself. I know what I did, and I deserve how he's treating me. It's a total cop-out to think that way, but I couldn't care less. As terrible as he is, I do love him and will do anything to prove it. Even if that means degrading myself. Love is a wicked thing.

I walk to the kitchen but stop in my tracks when I make it through the doorway. Lucas is sitting alone at the counter with a glass in front of him filled with amber liquid. Whiskey if I had to guess. He is quietly swirling the glass, listening to the clinking of the ice cubes.

I turn to back out, but he catches me. "Charlie. Wait. Please."

I'm not sure if it's the pain in his voice that turns me around or the desperation not to be alone, but against my better judgment and Teddy's warning, I do. "What?" I snap.

"We need to talk." He pats the stool next to him.

I huff and lean against the doorjamb. "There is nothing to talk about, Lucas."

He takes a swig of his drink, gulping the last of the liquid in his mouth and swallowing before he turns back to me. "There is. You can spend the rest of your life hating me, or you can listen to what I have to say."

I push off the jamb and go to walk away. "I'd rather hate you."

I wish I could tell him it's only for his own good—*our own good*—but I can't. If he thinks I hate him, it'll be easier on both of us. Sure, I never loved Lucas, but I did have feelings for him. He helped me see the light in a dark time. He became the friend I never expected to have. Someone who kept the memory of Teddy alive for me in a way.

I only make it a few steps before his hand is grabbing my elbow and hauling me back. He turns me to look at him again, then brings his face an inch from mine. "Hate me, Flower, I couldn't give a fuck less. But you need to realize *he* was the one who told me what to do. My loyalty lies far deeper with him than it does you. If you want to hate someone, hate him," he growls.

I swallow and scowl at him. "Don't get it wrong, I hate him

too." I wince at the words because maybe they are true. Love and hate run hand in hand, and sometimes it's hard to distinguish the difference. Or maybe I just hate who he is now.

I shake the thoughts away and continue. "But he wasn't the one trying to fuck me while I mourned. How low do you have to be to go that far, pretty boy?"

He leans his head back and cackles at my question. "So, you're a liar *and* a whore. If I'm remembering correctly, you're the one who kissed me. I'm the one who stopped it."

His words hurt, but I don't let it show on my face. He's right. I'm a liar. But I thought if I said it out loud and he somehow believed it, then I could believe it and feel better. Not feel the crushing weight of all the guilt alone.

I tilt my chin and listen as he continues.

"Boss was out of the picture, so you had to hop to the next. Tell me, baby, do you get off sucking his dick when he treats you like shit? Or is it just fucking men who murder? Knowing the pussy between your legs, the only thing you're good for, can drive them so mad they'd kill for you? Is that why you wanted me?"

His words mixed with the whiskey on his breath make me sick as the realization dawns on me. "You saw—"

He doesn't let me finish. "Oh, I saw it a*ll*. How you gagged and drooled as he shoved his cock into your throat. How he grabbed your hair so you couldn't move. Does that light another fire in you? Knowing I saw it all?"

I don't answer. Humiliation crawls all over my body. Lucas watched Teddy use me. Even worse, I let Teddy use me. My cheeks burn hot as my mouth goes dry.

"Don't worry. Your secret is safe with me. But I'm telling you now. Don't. Fucking. Cross. Me. I'll show you how murderous someone can get over your fucking cunt."

Once he leaves the kitchen, I gasp for the air that's left my lungs and sink to the floor. I'm stuck in a triangle I never intended to create or wanted to be in, and I have a feeling someone is going to die because of it.

The slamming of the door wakes me. I bolt upright in the bed and glance behind me. No light shines through the thin curtains, so it still has to be night. I stand from the bed and slip on my robe before walking to my door and cracking it open.

Teddy is already halfway down the hall, his eyes catching mine as he shuffles toward me. I step back into my room and leave the door open, waiting for him.

He walks in and closes the door quietly behind him. I'm not sure why considering the slam from the front was already probably heard by everyone.

"We have a problem," he states.

I tip my head. "What kind of problem?"

He shakes his head and starts pacing the floor in front of me. "Lucas got a call that someone was at the warehouse snooping around."

"Okay? It shouldn't matter because after you went away, I moved things around. The guns, the crates, everything that you had originally stored in the warehouse, has been relocated. It's just an empty building."

"I know that. It's more the fact of *who* was snooping around." He stops pacing.

"Who?"

"An ATF agent."

My heart skips a beat with his words. We may have the cops here on our side, or the chief at least, but the ATF is nothing more than an outsider. Someone who'll be harder to pay off.

"They can't be here without an invitation or cause. We haven't done anything in the light, so that means someone invited them."

The words almost stick in the back of my throat. What if Chief Sloan isn't who we think? He's the only one with enough jurisdiction other than…

"Cameron. Cameron brought them here."

Teddy stops pacing and looks at me. "Why do you say that?"

I walk back to my bed and sit on the edge before pulling open the nightstand drawer. I reach for the files and grip them, then toss it to Teddy. "That's why. He knows something, or is hiding something, and now he's trying to cover his ass. That's the only logical explanation. I mean, why would Sloan pull some shit like that."

Teddy flips through it. "Lucas told me about this. Did you talk to Cameron about it?"

My mind rewinds to that very moment, the night I learned

Teddy was alive, and all of my emotions come rushing back. Joy. Confusion. Anger.

I shake my head. "I was going to address it the night you came back. We made it to the station, but Lucas made a comment that threw me off guard, so we came home."

His jaw ticks with my mention of Lucas. "What did he say?" he grinds out.

I'm hesitant to repeat what Lucas said. I don't want to piss Teddy off especially since this isn't even about that, but I know he'll be angrier if I try and brush it off. "He said, because you mean something to him, you mean everything to me."

He nods, trying his best to act unfazed. "I will have the twins get with Emil. We can move our supply there. He'll watch it. And you, go talk to Cameron and see what we can find out. Don't let him or anyone else know I'm back. We will need the element of surprise."

"Emil? You can't be serious. I don't think we should trust him. He thinks you're dead—, what's keeping him from stealing everything for himself?"

"Just do as I say, Charlotte. I have an idea."

His words almost have a soft edge to them. Like he's tired of fighting. And honestly, I am too. I nod and reach for the files to put them back, but his grip doesn't release.

He pulls me forward using the file. His face is less than an inch from mine, and I can feel his breath fan across my lips. "You do mean something to me, Monkshood."

I want to melt at his words and crash into him, but the

guilt weighing in my stomach won't let me. "I know," I whisper, reaching for his face and running my thumb along his scar.

He presses his hand over mine and kisses my palm. "Don't ever forget you're mine."

How could I when I know if I do, someone will pay the price with their life? I want to say it, but I don't. "Yours," I breathe.

"Stop doing that," he spits, tugging my lip from my teeth.

I didn't even realize what I was doing. When he's so close to me, it's like my world turns to mush and all logic is thrown out the window. My body works on its own without the company of my brain. I breathe in deep, letting the need in my pants sound out around us.

"I should hate you," I whisper as he brings his face closer to mine.

"You should. It would make this whole thing easier."

"Maybe I do."

"You don't." He lets go to undo the button on his slacks and slips his suit jacket off his shoulders.

He walks me backward before laying me on the bed, letting the gun in his holster tickle my ribs as it hangs to his side. I reach up and push it down, but he pins my arms above me. Once my hands are where he wants them, he lets go and thumbs the buttons of his shirt open one by one. I watch in complete awe. Sure, I'm pissed at Teddy for… for everything, but I'd be lying if I said I didn't have an itch only he can scratch.

Once the last button is open, I expect him to take it off along with his holster, but he doesn't. He leaves both in place as he pushes down the band of his boxers and his erection is set free.

He grips his length and strokes himself slowly. "I've waited weeks to be back inside you," he breathes before letting his head loll back.

"Then what are you waiting on now?" I move my feet and hook my heels on the edge of the bed, letting the bottom of my robe fall open.

His head snaps back to me. After he eyes me, he lets out a husky laugh. "Not a damn thing. You can be mad, but it won't stop me from fucking you."

I smirk and raise an eyebrow, daring him to keep his word.

He smiles too, his real, genuine smile, then reaches for my panties and rips them off me with a growl. His head dives between my knees, his lips covering my thighs in punishing kisses and bites. I scream out from the mix of pain and pleasure and grind my core into his face. I do my best not to move my hands, but it's all too much.

The pain, the bliss, the fact that Teddy is even here, and… the guilt.

I push his head away from me and flip myself. Bringing my knees under me, I put my ass in the air and wait for him to have his way with me. As much as I want this—want him—I can't bear to look at him. Because of what I did, and what he did to me, but here I am, letting him use me again.

He dips his head and gives me one last painstakingly slow lick before standing back to his full height, centering himself and pounding into my pussy.

Over and over he pushes into me with zero care. He's doing it to find a release, and I'm looking at it as my punishment. He may not know I kissed Lucas, but the fact I know alone eats me alive. I need him to hurt me. I need him to use me.

He finally comes with a roar that shakes me to the core. Once he slows behind me and pulls out, I collapse onto the bed and cover my face. I don't want him to see the tears or read the guilt most definitely painted all over my face.

I hear the sound of his zipper, then the buckle of his belt being put in place, but I make no motion to move. I feel his body hover over mine as he plants a soft kiss in my hair. "I've missed you this way, my love." His voice is hoarse and weak.

When I don't reply, he tugs my arm from my face and sits me up. Tears smear down my cheeks as my lips quiver. His hard eyes grow soft. "What's the matter? Did I hurt you?"

Only in the way I deserve. I answer in my head. "No. I just—" I lick my lips and inhale deeply, trying to calm my nerves. "I missed you."

He nods and wraps his arms around me. "I know."

His words stir something in me. One minute, he was a savage, taking what he wanted without apology. And now, he's soft and sweet. Teddy is my very own Jekyll and Hyde, but I'm the only one who gets to see him soft.

I nuzzle my face into his neck and wrap my arms around his waist. "I just need to hold you for a second. To really feel you so I know this is real."

His body tenses under me before relaxing. He runs his hands through my hair and sways slowly, giving me only the second I wanted before he steps back in my hold. "I have to go, Monkshood."

I drop my arms and look up to him. I almost feel I'm looking at an entirely new man. Since he's been back, he's been so hot and cold, and I'm not sure if I want to burn or freeze.

He kisses the top of my head. "I'll be back. Until then, go see the pig and do whatever you must to get answers."

I nod at his command and watch him walk out my door.

CHAPTER SIX

Charlie

I let the day pass before I came to the station. No need to cause a scene in broad daylight. With it being past eight o'clock, most citizens would be home with their families by now, leaving only a few stray officers patrolling the streets. This way it'll leave no one but Sloan or Cameron at the station with the few dispatchers tucked away in the back.

Tonight, I came alone. Teddy is off doing god knows what, and I didn't want the twins or Carl shadowing me. One, I don't want to make anyone more nervous than they should be, walking in with three men who don't know the definition of play nice. And two, I'm trying to keep my distance with Lucas. Without a doubt I know Teddy is the one who is responsible for his beat-up face and outburst toward me. I don't want to add any fuel to the already burning inferno that is Teddy's anger.

I step out of my car and close the door. The creaking hinges send out a high-pitched squeal into the night. I revel in the sound. This old GTO has been mine since I was sixteen. It's one of the only things I have left from my dad. I smooth out my dress and move my purse to my shoulder.

I've been here a million and one times growing up, but this time isn't the same. I'm not here bearing a late dinner or exciting news; tonight I'm here to find answers so I can finally avenge my father.

I push through the doors and take in the small space. It's dimmer than normal with the overhead fluorescent lights cut down. A desk with the police seal on the front is to my left, a small room behind it filled with computers and a couple of people with headsets. A single holding cell in the back-right corner, and desks and computers scattered in the center.

I spot Sloan hunched over a desk, going through paperwork, with a lamp flipped on casting a dull yellow hue around him.

"Sloan," I state, stopping in front of his desk.

He looks up, startled. "Jesus, Charlie. You're going to give this old man a heart attack." He clutches his chest.

I don't bother with formalities. I get straight to the point. "Where's Snyder?"

He looks at the gold watch on his wrist before he darts his eyes back to me. "He left yesterday evening. Was supposed to be back for the night shift, but…" He stretches his arms around the empty room.

I chew on my lip. "Well, I'm waiting until he gets here." I plop onto the chair next to his desk.

He raises his eyebrow. "What's going on, Charlie?" I can hear a hint of concern in his voice.

I huff. "Family business, Chief."

As much as I want to give him all the information I have, I don't even know if I can trust him. He's worked alongside Cameron as long as he did my dad. Sure, he helps Teddy with small things here and there, but who's to say he isn't helping Cameron too? I can't risk spilling the small info I have and him running with it.

He shakes his head and rolls his eyes. "I see those boys are finally rubbing off on you. Teddy trained you well." His voice lowers and sounds almost pained. "It's a shame he isn't here to see it."

For a second his comment catches me off guard. I'd almost forgotten no one knows Teddy is back. That his entire death was a lie.

I look to the floor and feign grief, wiping a fake tear from my cheek. "Let's not go there. Please," I beg, hoping my pitiful excuse of hurt will fool him.

He nods in understanding before patting my back and walking to the small room tucked away at the front of the station. Relief floods me when he's out of sight. I almost feel guilty lying to Sloan. He's been nothing but a rock to me for so long. When my dad couldn't make it in time to pick me up from school, or knew he'd miss a dance recital, Sloan was always the man who took his place. He's been like a dad to me in a way, but the one thing I've learned over the past few months is people aren't who they seem. Lies and deception linger beneath the surface for everyone. It's just a matter of what they're covering up. I can't risk letting Sloan in, letting him know what's going on.

The door opening grabs my attention. I look and see Cameron strolling in, dressed in a wrinkled uniform with his sandy hair a mess. Sloan appears from the dispatch room where they exchange a few words before he walks out the door.

I stand, making sure the strap of my bag is still in place on my shoulder. When Cameron doesn't notice me, I make my presence known. "Snyder," I call out softly, not wanting the few women in the dispatch room to hear me.

His hazel eyes meet mine and immediately light up. "Charlotte." He smiles, wasting no time to shrink the space between us.

He stops in front of me, his worn work boots almost stepping on my toes. He leans in, no doubt to kiss me like he does every time he sees me, but I back away.

When the back of my knees hit the edge of the chair, I hold up my hand. I'm done playing nice with this prick. "You're going to tell me what you know."

His eyes flash darkly before he slips his fake friendly mask back in place. "What are you talking about?"

I reach in my bag and pull out his file I found in my dad's storage unit. I throw it on the desk, then reach back inside and grab my gun. I sit back down and urge him to do the same with the chair opposite of me, nodding my head in its direction. I cross one leg over the other, then lean back, removing my hand from my bag and letting it rest in my lap.

Cameron reaches for the file, keeping his eyes on my gun the entire time. He flips through it, then looks to me with bewilderment in his eyes. "What's this?"

"You tell me." I keep my voice impassive. No need to give him any hints that I have no clue what it means. All I know is he knows. But what does he know is the real question here. My dad didn't leave that answer.

He shakes his head, then throws the file back onto the desk. "I don't know what any of that is."

I take in a deep breath through my nose, then stand up quickly. I lean over him. The sick fuck can't even look into my eyes. He's too worried about sneaking a peek down the low dip of the front of my dress.

I drag my gun up his knee to his thigh and let it rest by his groin. With the barrel pointed directly at his dick, I click the safety off. "You know something, Cameron, and I want to know what. And I want to know why there's an ATF agent snooping around my warehouse."

He leans his head back and lets out a sinister laugh while grinding into my gun slightly. "Look at you, Charlie. Finally, you have some steel in that floppy backbone. Maybe fucking all those Hale men did you some good. Is that how you got to claim that old run-down warehouse as yours too?" His face contorts achingly like he didn't mean to say what he did.

I laugh. How weak. If you're going to say something, say it without apology. "What, jealous it wasn't you? That it wasn't your hands skimming all over my naked body. Not your cock pushing into me, making me cry out in ecstasy?" His lip flicks up, and his hands ball into fists in his lap.

I moan into his ear. "Upset I wasn't screaming out your name?" I flick my tongue over the shell of his ear. I can see the bulge growing in his pants. Good. He's right where I want him.

Lucas said the only thing I'm good for is my pussy, and maybe in a way he's right. I can make men do things other men can't. I can use my body and the fantasy of sex to get what I want. Teddy said it best. Where a man can't go, he'll send a woman.

I stand back straight and put my foot on the edge of the chair between his legs. I give him a seductive smirk before pushing as hard as I can, sending him falling to the floor. I stand over him and aim my gun at his head. "Next time I come, you'll have answers. And as far as the warehouse, it's none of your fucking business. It's mine and that's all you need to know."

I turn and walk out of the station before he can ask anything more.

CHAPTER SEVEN

Cameron

I watch as Charlie sways out of the station. As much as I want to stop her, I don't. The way her hips move as she walks with authority, her hands gliding beside her with her gun still gripped in one. Everything about her screams confidence, and it's a look I haven't seen her wear in a while. Maybe those Hale men have done one good thing for her. They've built her up and made her see just how amazing she is. They've taken away some of the work for me. When Charlie is finally with me, where she belongs, she'll be exactly who I want her to be.

As the door closes behind her, I scramble from the floor and stand, pulling my phone from my pocket, and dial Andrew's number.

When the phone connects, I don't wait for a hello. "Meet me in the back of the station. *Now.*" I end the call before he can reply.

I see Andrew's headlights splash through the doors as he pulls up and parks right in front of the station. I shake my head and roll my eyes, then walk outside. As he's stepping out of his car, I grab him by the arm and haul him to the back of the building.

Once we're covered by the night and too far away for anyone to hear, I face him. "I said meet me in the back. What the fuck are you doing?"

He jerks from my hold and straightens his jacket. "First of all, I don't work for you. I will do what I want."

I pinch the bridge of my nose and squeeze my eyes so tight I see spots. "If you want to be here and get the big break you're looking for, so your boss will take you off of administrative leave, you'll do as I say. Not being discreet isn't an option."

He chuckles. "I'm sure you need me just as badly as I need you. If this is going to work, I need to be able to work without parameters."

I want to pummel his face and show him just how serious I am, but I can't because he's right. I do need him. I have no evidence against the Hales, and trying to find any is almost impossible. They know who I am, and I'm sure they already have eyes on me. I can't risk looking into anything and getting caught.

"Just try to lay low. They already know you're here which

can be problematic. Watch your back if you run into them. They're good at what they do and know how to cover things up."

"Oh, like you?" He chuckles wickedly.

"Fuck off, Andrew. Just do what you need to do to get them thrown away. I have people waiting to get to them behind bars."

He shakes his head and starts to walk away. "Whatever."

I follow and watch as he gets into his car and leaves. I hurry inside and hope like hell erasing the past ten minutes of footage from the cameras that watch the front of the station won't be too suspicious.

CHAPTER EIGHT

Charlie

I walk inside and drop my purse to the floor. The thump echoes off the marble, alerting Carl to my presence. His head peeks out of the kitchen before retreating again.

I walk to the kitchen and plop onto the barstool across the counter of where he is. "Where is he?"

I don't give an explanation. He knows who I'm talking about.

Carl shakes his head, his white hair moving the slightest bit with the motion. "Not here, but he did tell me you and the boys will be going to see Emil."

I look to the counter where his hands have been moving. He's arranging fancy cheese and meats into plastic baggies, then placing them into a small wicker basket.

"Is this for him?" I ask, pointing to the arrangement.

He nods. "His favorite is the smoked sausage links and old dutch master gouda. Most pair the cheese with sweets because of its flavor, but not Emil." He shakes his head like he's disappointed. "Such a waste to not enjoy its flavor to its full potential, but what can I say?"

I scoff at his comment. Only Carl would get bent out of shape over some old cheese. "Why do you care so much, Carl?"

He stops shuffling the full baggies in the basket around, then looks up to me. "I don't care for Emil, but I do care for Teddy and the boys. They're young and don't realize the power of their words sometimes. I figure if I can show Emil he's appreciated, just for the simple fact of not killing us, I will. Those Hale men sure won't. They're too proud and talk a lot of shit, but I've been around longer than them. Sometimes you have to put your pride to the side."

"You really think Emil would kill them just because they aren't his family?"

"I do. I've seen it happen. What Emil is doing is unheard of in this world. Competition over territory and who is supreme is a big thing, and no one likes losing."

I nod, understanding what he's saying the best I can. Before I can reply, Lucas and Julius stroll in.

"You rolling too, Carl?" Lucas asks, completely ignoring me and acting like I'm not sitting right in front of him.

"Yes. Here." He passes the basket to me before turning to the fridge and pulling out a bottle of wine. "Take this to him when you go in."

"I thought you guys were going to handle this," I remark, tipping my head as he passes the bottle to me.

"You're the face of this family now, Charlotte. It's best if you do it."

I glance to Lucas and Julius, who stand quietly next to me, then back to Carl. "Well, let's go."

The ride to Emil's casino was awkward. Julius was quiet, as always, and Carl stayed in his own world, swaying to the low soft jazz he turned on. Lucas, normally one to talk shit or make smart-ass remarks, did nothing. When his eyes would catch mine, he'd hurry to look away disgusted. And if I happened to accidentally brush against him going over a bump, he'd make a show of scooting closer to his brother.

The tension between him and me is something I haven't ever experienced, and it makes my stomach turn. He used to be a friend. A shitty friend, but a friend, nonetheless.

I push the thoughts away and chastise myself for even thinking about that shit. Why do I care? It isn't like I love him, not how I love Teddy at least. The love I have for Lucas is a different kind, more of a brotherly love. The kind of love you give to the guy who isn't good enough for any woman because they're loud, obnoxious, too full of themselves. The pretty boys who don't want to settle down.

Once the twins exit the car, I follow behind them through

the parking lot, holding the basket Carl insisted on sending loose at my side. Neon lights bounce off the shiny pavement, throwing splashes of blue, yellow, and green into the dark night.

Closer to the entrance, they slow their pace and flank my sides as I survey totally new surroundings. A golden archway covered in small flashing red lights hangs over the revolving glass door. A giant sign that reads *Hideout* hangs down the red brick, while lines of blue and green dance beside it.

I pause for a minute and watch the people who are coming in and out. No one really stands out. Mainly men in suits shuffle along with the occasional woman in a fancy dress breaking up all of the testosterone.

I continue inside, completely awed as soon as I step in. The lights across the entire building are dim, minus the small, single-hanging chandeliers over every blackjack and poker table and the lights flashing on the slot machines.

I nudge my chin forward, looking at Julius, telling him to lead the way. He weaves between tables and cocktail waitresses dressed in lingerie until he reaches the very back of the casino.

Emil sits at a lone table with a woman on each side of him. One blonde, one brunette, each covering his neck in kisses and whispering in his ear. "Charlotte, what a surprise."

I nod. "Emil."

Julius and Lucas spread out, taking guard on each side of the table as I sit down in front of him. I place the basket on the table. "Carl says hello."

A smile stretches his lips as he reaches for it. "That man

knows me too well," He laughs, digging through the bags. "What can I do for you, Charlie?"

I swallow down all of my uncertainty and the fact I think this is a terrible idea, then speak. "I need a favor."

He leans up, putting his elbows on the table top with an even bigger smile. "You need my help? I never thought this day would come."

You and me both. "There is an ATF agent snooping around my warehouse. He won't find anything because I've kept things at the house, but soon enough I'm sure he'll come there. I need somewhere to put all of the guns, somewhere safe."

His eyes widen before he leans back into his chair and drapes his arms over the women at his side. "So, you need me to hold your supply? How long?"

I look to Julius, then Lucas for answers, for the right thing to say, but they give me nothing. Carl's words ring out in my head *"You're the face of this family now."*

I take a deep breath and try and muster up every ounce of bravado I have. "However long it takes to get him off our case. Are you going to help me or not?" I lean back and cross one knee over the other, acting placid when I'm anything but that.

If he doesn't help, I don't know what else to do. Sure, Teddy will figure it out, but I don't want to have to face him and tell him I failed.

"Fair enough." He pulls the women closer to him. "I'll send Desi over tomorrow to pick everything up."

"I want to know where they'll be, and I want access at all

times," I state, standing up.

"Do you not trust me, Charlie?" He sounds almost wounded, and it makes me want to laugh.

I smooth out my dress and motion for the twins. "Quite frankly, I don't, and you know it, but I'm out of options here."

He shakes his head with a smirk. "I guess I can admire your honesty."

I turn and start walking to the front without another word because I don't feel he deserves it.

We only make it to the center of the casino before a blonde bombshell is pressing herself against Lucas.

"Oh, I've missed you, Luke," she breathes in his ear.

I can tell he's uncomfortable by the way his body tenses and his eyes narrow, but he quickly replaces it when his eyes grab mine.

He hooks his arm around her slim waist and pulls her even closer, letting her tits push into his side. "Have you now, Jade?"

He flicks his eyes to her and roams them all over her half-naked body. As I watch them, my breaths become coarser and my stomach gets heavy. I don't even know who she is, but I want to rip her away from him and throw her on her ass.

I cross my arms over my center and roll my eyes. "We need to go. Now."

I turn on my heel and start walking toward the door again, quickening my pace. I feel Julius rush up beside me, but I don't pay him any attention. Suddenly, the only thing I can think about is putting an adequate distance between me and Lucas.

I make it to the car and throw the door open before sliding inside. Julius lingers by the door until Lucas finally appears. He slips in next to me, and suddenly, I feel suffocated. I don't want him near me.

"Get out," I say low, hoping Carl and Julius don't hear.

He tips his head. "Why?"

I feel the air crash through my teeth as I turn toward the window away from him, seething at the thought of him being so close. "I don't want you near me. Get out and let Julius in first or walk home. Your choice."

I can't see his face, but I can picture him with the same look he had in the kitchen the other night. "Fine."

The weight of him suddenly leaves the seat and is quickly replaced when the car door closes. Carl doesn't take off right away like normal, but I don't question it. I just keep my eyes glued out the window.

After a few moments, the car shifts into gear and we're gliding across the parking lot, onto the main road back home. Once we're a good distance away from the casino and all of its flashing lights, I sneak a peek beside me and only see Julius.

"Where the fuck is Lucas?"

Julius shrugs with a grin, looking to Carl through the rearview mirror.

"He chose to walk." Carl shakes his head, then turns the music louder.

CHAPTER NINE

Teddy

I spent the whole night watching Cameron at the station. He doesn't know it, but I saw him. Dirty pig not only met with the ATF agent, but he also went in and tampered with the security camera. And I also saw Charlie. Seeing her act so strong and unafraid did nothing but remind me of the many reasons why I love her. Why she's my fucking queen.

I slip back into my car and start the engine. The station doesn't have much around it, so I parked across the street in hopes of not being seen. Luckily, not many people in Northridge Heights think twice about a basic car sitting in a lone parking lot at night. It's the whole reason I went and bought this little Honda.

I pull onto the street, still watching the inside of the station until I'm too far away to see. Once I'm out of sight, I flip on my lights and head back to the house. I've been staying outside of town in a run-down motel so I don't cross anyone's path, but now that Charlie knows I'm back, it's too hard to stay away. Sure, she may be mad at me, but I know she feels the same way. I can see it in her eyes, her body language, the way she speaks. She missed me as much as I missed her.

I pull into the drive and lower my head so the hat I'm wearing covers my face as I approach the guard shack. I made the boys get rid of everyone we used to have stationed here and only kept the two I felt we could halfway trust. But I still don't trust them enough to know I'm back. Carl made sure to instruct them when my car pulls up to not ask questions and to let me in, so they do.

I park next to Charlie's old GTO and step out. Leaning against my car, I wait.

After a few minutes, headlights snake up the drive and creep in slowly. Once the engine is killed, Carl steps out of the driver's seat followed by Julius and then Charlie from the back. Lucas isn't to be seen, but I don't question it. After all the bullshit that's been going on, I'm not complaining either. The less time he's around Charlie, the better.

Charlie goes to walk up the steps but stops when she sees me. "Teddy." She dips her head as she approaches.

"Monkshood." I reach out for her and grab her waist, pulling her into me and inhaling the scent of her hair. "Did you talk to Cameron?"

I already know the answer, but I want to see how much she'll tell me. I don't know what was said, but I saw what she did, and after everything with Lucas, I just need a reason to give her my full trust again.

"I did and didn't get anything useful." Her head falls.

I tip her chin so she's facing me. "Don't worry, I have a plan."

"Care to enlighten us?" Carl chirps from behind her.

I drop my hand and move behind her. "Whoever was with Cameron that day at the bank is in with the cartel. I have a feeling he's the one running things. I've seen him too much for it to be a coincidence. If we can figure out exactly who he is, that's one problem handled. As far as the ATF agent, I know Cameron brought him into town. Basically, everything goes back to the pig. We need to get him alone and get answers."

"I've already tried that," Charlie remarks, crossing her arms over her chest.

"I know, but now we have a little on him. If we can figure out how he's connected to this other man, then maybe we can use it against him."

"And how do you intend to do that?"

I laugh. She obviously underestimates my ability to get info. As long as you have a small piece of something, everything else comes easy. People don't call me devious for nothing. I have ways of getting what I want.

"The ATF agent obviously isn't here with the support of where he came from because he's alone. I'm sure he knows more than us. If we can give him a new lead to follow, maybe he'll reward our generosity with some intel."

She tips her head and chews her lip. "And where are we going to find a new lead?"

I ignore her question and answer it with my own. "Did Emil agree to hold our supply?"

She nods. "Desi will be here tomorrow to pick up."

"Good." I look at Carl and Julius. "Get everything ready to be moved tomorrow, then rest up. I'll elaborate more later." I look back to Charlie as they disappear inside. "Make sure you go with him tomorrow and have easy access. Memorize the layout the best you can too or anything that could be problematic."

Her eyes widen. "You aren't thinking of doing what I think you are—"

I hold up my hand. "Don't overanalyze anything just yet. We will talk tomorrow."

I kiss the top of her head and kick myself when she flinches the slightest bit. As much as I hate that she's scared of me, I don't regret anything I've said or done up until this point.

Loving a woman is new to me. Sure, I've had flings, but it's different with Charlie. The thought of her with anyone else makes me insane. I know Lucas would never betray me, but at the same time, Charlie has my head all fucked-up. If I'm able to see how great she is, I'm sure everyone else can see it too. Including Lucas.

The way her body moves with authority and sweetness all in the same strut. How her voice is calm and hypnotic but demanding too. Everything about her screams anomaly but perfectly right in the same breath. Charlie will be the fucking death of me.

I push the thought away and wish her a good night before getting back into my car and leaving.

CHAPTER TEN

Charlie

When Teddy left last night, my mind wouldn't stop racing. I'm almost sure I know what he has planned, and I know it isn't a good idea. I try to halt my thoughts and focus on getting ready. Desi should be here soon.

I look at myself in the mirror and smooth down my tank top. I'm sure Desi is harmless, at least right now, but I want to be prepared for anything. I push my feet into my tennis shoes and leave my room, gliding into the kitchen.

"Good morning, Charlotte." Carl beams from one side of the counter.

"Morning. Can I get some of that?" I point to the french press next to him.

He nods and pours me a glass, adding two scoops of sugar. When he hands me the cup, I wrap my hands around it and blow on the steam coming from the top and let my mind wander even more to what Teddy is planning.

"What's the matter?" Carl asks.

I drag my eyes to him. I can't be positive Teddy is going to do what I think, so I don't tell him. I sigh internally when I realize I'm doing it again. Protecting the man I love when he probably doesn't even deserve it. Protecting is probably a strong word to use in this instance considering he doesn't need protecting from Carl, but it still fits in a sense. I'm keeping his unspoken secrets.

"I don't know. I guess I'm just still fucked-up by the fact Teddy is alive, and I'm not sure how I'm supposed to feel." The confession almost feels good. Finally stating a true-to-me fact lifts a weight off my shoulders I didn't even know I was carrying. But at the same time, I don't think Carl would understand. He isn't my friend, he's Teddy's. He's loyal to Teddy.

He nods, circling the counter to sit next to me. "Be mad as hell. That's how you should feel. Your feelings are valid and just when it comes to him. Teddy may have a point to prove, but you can't let him see you weak while he does it."

I sip my coffee, then look at him. "What do you mean by a point to prove?"

He grins at me like I'm stupid and grips my shoulder. "Now Charlotte, don't act stupid. Everyone can see what's going on between you and Lucas clear as day. You remember what I said about pride? Teddy almost has too much of it. He feels he has to prove a point right now, show everyone you're his."

My heart sinks with his words, and suddenly, I feel completely humiliated. How is it so easy for everyone to see whatever the fuck is going on between me and Lucas, Teddy included, other than me?

He pats my knee. "Don't worry. All of that shit will get worked out eventually. Men like Teddy don't love easily, and when they do, it drives them crazy. Everything he's doing is out of love even though it may not seem like it."

Maybe Carl has a point, but I don't get long to ponder on it. Julius comes into the kitchen freshly showered with his hair still wet and slicked back. He has on dark-washed jeans and a plain black tee.

"Are you coming with me today?" He nods as a knock comes from the front door. "Okay then. Let's get this done."

I stand from the barstool and exit the kitchen. When I make it to the door, I take one last deep breath and tell myself I can handle whatever comes my way.

I pull open the door and see Desi standing on the other side. Just like the few times I've seen him before, he's wearing a button-down shirt and slacks and has silver jewelry covering his fingers and neck.

"Charlotte. Buenos días, hermosa." He reaches for my hand and kisses the top.

"Good morning, Desi. I have everything ready to move." I motion to the crates beside the door that Carl and Julius moved down here last night.

He nods as two men dressed in all black appear from behind him and start grabbing crates with Julius. One after the other, they load them into a plain white van with blacked-out windows.

Once the last crate is loaded, I walk down the steps and slip into Desi's waiting car with Julius and Desi behind me.

We drive to the south side of town, Emil's territory, winding down narrow and unmarked roads. After what feels like forever, we pull up to an abandoned-looking shack. The blue paint is peeling off the distressed wood, the porch hangs lower on the right side, and the grass covering the lawn is overgrown.

The tires crunch over the gravel drive a few feet, then stop with the van directly behind us. Everyone exits the car. Desi goes straight up the sketchy steps while the two goons follow him as Julius and I linger by the car.

"I really don't like this," I mumble to myself.

"I don't either." Julius's voice comes out low and raspy.

I turn to my side with wide eyes. "Are you actually talking to me?"

A smile forms on his lips. "I am."

I prop my hand on my hip. "Huh. I knew you had a voice, but I never thought you would use it in everyday life."

He scoffs. "You and I have never really gotten a chance to be alone. Normally, I only stay quiet to listen. Pick up all the things other people miss. Right now, it's only you and I, so there is no need to be quiet unless you want to tell me plans on world domination or some shit."

"Damn. And here I was thinking you took a vow of silence for a reason. You know, like a protest of your own for a cause you believe in." I shrug.

He shakes his head. "Nope. I mean, maybe it started that way. When my mom died, Lucas and I were left with our dad. He always got on to us about being too rambunctious. Too loud. He'd beat us until we were black and blue. So, one day I decided I'd show him exactly how quiet I could be. At first everything was fine, but after a while it had the opposite effect. He hated how I was too quiet. Man never could make up his fucking mind about what he wanted." He kicks the gravel beneath his feet.

I sigh quietly at his confession.

"Now"—he drags my attention back to him—"I just stay quiet because when I do speak, it actually makes an impact. Just look at how you reacted."

I raise my brow. "You're smarter than you look."

He shakes his head softly as Desi and the two men come back out of the house.

Desi stops in front of me. He reaches out his hand with a key between his fingers. "This will open the door." He reaches in his pocket and pulls out another key. "And this will open the shed back there."

He points behind the house. About fifty yards back sits a metal shop–looking building in pristine condition. It doesn't look like it belongs in the same vicinity as the run-down house. "Is that where you'll keep my guns?"

He nods. "Yes. No one knows we own this. It's completely untraceable back to us, which means it won't get back to you either. And as a show of good faith, Emil stored some of our important files there. Information on some of our biggest clients."

Guns are definitely the worse of the two, looking at things one-sided, but if you dig deeper into their sex rings, I'm sure big politicians, doctors, and lawyers use their services. It may be a good show of faith storing files with our things, but a stupid move. I would never incriminate myself for someone else, but I guess that's where Emil and I are different. He wants so badly to prove to me he cared for Teddy, but he's doing nothing but making reckless moves.

I chuckle and take both keys and start walking in the tall grass toward the shed while Julius follows.

When we make it to the entrance, Julius steps in front of me. "Let me go first and make sure this isn't a setup."

I nod and hand him the key.

Julius rolls open the door, revealing an almost bare shop. Dust coats the concrete floor with a few fresh tracks in it, leading to the four filing cabinets tucked into the corner. I step in behind him and look to the wall. Finding the light switch, I flip it on. Fluorescent lights buzz to life.

"Seems okay, I guess." I shrug. I'm still not convinced this is a good idea, but what can I do?

"We can set everything up in the back. It's a little drive, but at least they'll be safe and keep the ATF agent away. We can just make runs as we need things or clients come into town."

I nod, then look behind me. The goons and Desi are trekking through the tall grass toward us. Once they finally make it in front of me, I eye the two men. "You can unload here. This will work for now."

They look at me with a laugh before turning to Desi. Desi nods. "Do as she says. Bring the van back here and put everything where she wants."

I tip my head as they walk off sulking. "Another show of good faith, letting me boss your men around?"

"Not at all. You have to remember I've seen what you can do—I don't want none of that smoke."

I brush off the comment and flash Desi a fake smile. The van pulls up and turns, backing toward the door. The two men, Julius, and Desi get to work unloading all of the crates while I stand and watch and continue to scour the place for anything suspicious.

Once the last crate is stacked on the others in the back, I hop into the passenger side of the van. One of the men looks at me, and the confusion shines through. "I'm not walking back through that grass." He shakes his head and puts the van into drive as the other man, Julius, and Desi pile into the back.

We pull back onto the gravel drive in no time. I step out, thank the two men, then slip back into Desi's car with Julius following. Desi enters the front and starts the car silently.

As we drive back to our place, Julius stares out his window. I debate on starting a conversation but think better of it. I have a feeling he's done all the talking he'd like for now.

As we broach the gates of home, I unhook my seat belt and lean forward. "Thank you, Desiderio. We will talk soon."

He nods as I leave the car and head inside.

CHAPTER ELEVEN

Cameron

It's been days since Andrew got here, and he still hasn't found anything to pin down the Hales.

I reach in my pocket and dial his number. When the call connects, I start speaking. "Any news? My patience is wearing thin."

I hear a loud sigh on the other end. "Nothing yet. I've talked to the owners surrounding their warehouse, I've watched the girl, I even tried to talk to people at the bank. Without warrants I can't do anything, and being on leave, I can't get the warrants I need."

I grip my hair and tug it. "She'll lead you to their supply. Keep watching her."

"I have been, but someone else has caught my interest—"

I cut him off. "This isn't about anyone else. This is about those fucking Hales. I want them gone, Andrew! I didn't bring you here to look into anyone else."

The line is quiet for a moment before he speaks again. "Fine." He hangs up.

I squeeze my phone, then throw it to my side. "You need to leave town, David."

David looks at me with a smirk. "You think I'm scared of them?"

"Don't make this about how big and bad you are, this isn't what that's about. They have the chief on their side and more resources than me. If they want you dead, then you'll be dead."

He paces the floor in my apartment lazily like he can't be bothered with what I'm saying. "Chill out, cousin. Sebastian wouldn't let anything happen to me. You may not have much, but he has all of Mexico on his side. I'm not worried."

I stand from my couch and grab him by the shoulders. "That's the fucking problem! This isn't Mexico, David. He doesn't have the same kind of pull here. Stop being so fucking stupid and listen to what I'm saying."

I wish I could shake him hard enough till he understood, but David hears nothing. He's stubborn and strong-willed, only believing what he wants.

"Stop acting like my mamá. I will handle them if they try anything."

I roll my eyes and plop back onto my couch. He is going to get killed and doesn't even care.

CHAPTER TWELVE

Charlie

As I walk inside, I see Teddy standing in the foyer. "Did you get everything moved?"

I nod. "Yeah. They're keeping it on the southside, about thirty minutes from the casino."

"What kind of building? Any security?"

Before I can answer, a knock vibrates through the foyer. I look to Teddy with confusion. The same expression on my face mirrors on his. He holds his finger to his lips and moves behind the door.

I nod and reach for the handle. When I open it a man in his late thirties is standing on the other side. "Can I help you?"

"Charlotte Welsh?" His voice is deep.

I lean against the open door and weigh my words carefully.

"It's actually Hale. And you are?"

"My name is Andrew Scott. I'm in town investigating some claims and was wanting to ask you a few questions."

Bingo. I knew it had to be him, the ATF agent. Growing up in this town, I know almost every face. Maybe not names, but I know faces, and this is one I haven't seen before.

"Oh, a real investigation? What kind of claims?" I peek behind the door and see Teddy listening just as intently as me for his reply.

"I can't disclose that information right now."

I huff. "So, you're here to ask me questions, about something you can't *disclose*? Sounds to me you're just fishing for anything I'm willing to give. Have a nice day." I look behind me and see Julius standing with an amused smirk plastered on his face, chin jutted upward and his arms crossed over his chest.

I go to close the door, but he stops it with his foot. "I'm a government agent with the ATF. If you don't cooperate, I can have you arrested for obstruction of a criminal investigation."

Julius moves closer behind me, pressing his chest into my back. I look behind the door and see Teddy watching, nostrils flaring, fists curling, because he can't do anything about this man trying to practically force himself inside. Not if he wants to keep him being back a secret.

I chuckle at his threat and step forward away from Julius. "Am I supposed to be scared because of who you are? I mean, I can't think of any other good reason as to why you would be so forward. Unless it's because you already know that I know who you are." I drop my hip and level my eyes with his. "And if you know who I am, the same way I know you, then you must know who my father was. I was learning the legal system and laws before I could walk. I'm not obstructing shit. So, unless you have a warrant, probable cause, or feel like spilling what you're actually investigating, go fuck yourself."

He takes a step back and raises his hands in surrender with a smug smile.

I shrug and chuckle again. "That's what I thought. Tell Cameron I said hello." I slam the door before he can reply.

When the door slams shut, Teddy steps forward. "That motherfucker!" he yells.

His booming voice penetrates every pore in my body, a wicked mixture of venom and ice, sending a chill down my spine. I've seen Teddy mad before, but never to the point of yelling.

"He has some fucking nerve trying to get into my home!" He walks to the small table by the door in two big strides. Picking up the golden vase housing lilies, he doesn't hold it for more than a second before throwing it down the hall.

The shattering of the glass on the marble floor has me jumping with the sound. I almost want to run away, but more than that, I want to try and comfort him. I rush to his side and touch his arm tentatively. "Teddy, it's okay. I handled it."

He snatches out of my hold. "That's the point, Charlotte. You shouldn't have to handle it with me standing right fucking there!" He points to the door. "You don't know how much it took not to step around you and pummel his face. He disrespected you!"

Warmth floods my body with his confession. I shake my head. "I'm used to it. One of my main advantages is people thinking I'm weak. People not taking me as serious. It's okay."

His head falls back as he lets out a laugh. "This isn't about weakness, Charlotte. You've already shown your weakness. Your composure wavers when a certain someone comes around." He leans down and brings his eyes to mine. "This is about disrespect. You called yourself a Hale, and he still had the nerve to do what he did. No one treats anyone with the Hale name that way and gets away with it. Don't think this is about you when it isn't. This is about my family's name and the reputation I've built with it."

My jaw becomes slack, and my hands start to shake. Just when I thought maybe we were past the Lucas thing, he brings it up again. I bite my lip so hard that the copper taste of blood touches my tongue. I want to fire back, but it's pointless.

I turn and see Lucas stepping out of his room as I start toward the hallway.

"What, running away because you can't handle the truth, Charlotte?" I hear Teddy call behind me.

My eyes catch Lucas's for a split second. He raises his brow slightly and tips his head, almost like he's waiting to see what I'll do, and it pisses me off. These men brought me here for my strength. They've groomed me and trained me to be hard and cold, and yet, Lucas has the nerve to look at me with pity in his eyes while Teddy talks shit.

I turn on my heel and storm back to Teddy. "Fuck you.

You want to say you're just a man questioning all he's done for a woman who doesn't love him the same way, but you know what? I'm questioning all the same shit too." I throw my hands up and raise my voice. "You want to prove a point that I'm yours? You've done it. Look at Lucas's bruised face and my fucking piss-poor excuse of dignity! I've let you treat me like shit the entire time you've been back thinking maybe you just needed to let it out. But fuck you, Theodore! I'm not your fucking doormat anymore.

"Nothing I've done deserves this kind of treatment. You're a prick on a power trip at this point, and I'm sick of it! If you want to treat someone like shit, find a new victim because I'm done being yours!"

I can see the anger brewing in his eyes the moment I finish. The corner of his mouth picks up in a grin, bunching the scar along his face. An evil, depraved, vicious grin. He inhales loudly through his nose, then lets it out quickly before raising his hand.

I close my eyes and wait for the impact, but it never comes.

I open my eyes slowly and look in front of me. I see the most beautiful but wayward thing. Lucas is standing behind Teddy, gripping his arm, while their eyes battle with unspoken words.

Julius steps up and watches them fixedly like he's ready for the war that's about to wage between them. I can see the indecisiveness pooling in his eyes, contemplating which side to take.

"You aren't this person, boss." Lucas finally breaks the

silence.

Like something clicks, Teddy lowers his hand, shoots his eyes to the ground, then storms outside without a word.

Once the door clicks closed behind him, I release a breath that's been stuck in my lungs. I close my eyes and breathe deep through my nose, then release it, taking a moment to compose myself. I walk to the hallway and drop to my knees, careful not to cut myself, then start picking up the biggest pieces of glass from the vase.

Carl comes from the kitchen with a broom and paper bag. My eyes catch his and immediately start to water when I see the pain in his. I drop the glass from my hands and lean back on my knees. "What am I doing wrong, Carl? I've done everything possible to show him I'm here for him. I'm his."

He shakes his head lightly, then sweeps the broom in front of me, pushing all of the glass in one pile. "That man is a different creature. An enigma if you will. What he does may not make sense to us, but it's perfectly coherent in his own mind. You just need to have patience with that devious king of yours, Charlotte."

A sad chuckle boils from my throat. "Patience? Seems like I need a bulletproof vest and skin of steel instead."

"You'll be okay, kid. Just give it time. From what I overheard, he's hitting his own turning point." He brushes all of the glass into the paper bag before folding the top and disappearing back into the kitchen.

Once he's out of sight, I stand and walk to my room. Once

I'm in the safety of my own space, I sink to the floor and replay everything in my mind. How can any of them think what Teddy is doing is normal? How can they justify it? Nothing in my world makes sense anymore, and I don't know how to piece it back together. How to make shit normal again.

CHAPTER THIRTEEN

Teddy

As much as I hate to admit it, Lucas was right last night. I'm not some lowlife piece of shit who hits women. So why was I raising my hand to Charlotte? I swore to protect her, but here I am, turning into her biggest threat.

I pace the floor of the run-down motel, my designer shoes scuffing the cheap tile. "Fuck this!" I say out loud to myself.

I turn toward the door and swing it open, then slip out and into my car. I put it in drive and floor it, letting the gravel kick up behind me and leave a trail of dust in my wake.

Before I turn into the drive, I pull the baseball cap on my head lower to cover my eyes. The guard at the gate, someone I haven't seen before, nods as he hits a button and the gate swings open. I pull in next to Charlie's old Pontiac and park. I take off my cap and throw it into the passenger seat before I exit.

Walking to the door, I contemplate if I really want to do what I've been thinking. Taking a deep breath, I walk inside and close the door behind me. "Boys!" I yell.

Lucas and Julius emerge from their rooms and strut until they're right in front of me. Lucas is the first to speak, as always. "What is it, boss?"

"I want you to call Sloan. Get him here now."

Lucas raises his eyebrow, looks to Julius, then back to me. "In case you've forgotten, you're still dead."

I scrub my hand down my face and try to tighten the top on the bottle of anger I have buried in me. I've already exploded multiple times; I don't need to do it again. "I said, call Sloan. *Now.*"

I'm not sure if it's the edge I make sure is present in my voice, or the fact Lucas knows he's on thin ice with me, but he pulls a phone from his pocket and dials Sloan's number.

"You." I point to Julius "Go get Charlie." He disappears without question.

"Hey, Chief." I listen as Lucas talks. "Yeah, everything is fine. I was wondering if you could stop by for a minute… No, everything is fine, like I said, we just have some business to discuss… Okay… Okay."

As he ends the call, Julius comes out of Charlie's room with her in tow. When they stop in front of me, her eyes don't meet mine. She hardly acknowledges my presence.

I shake away the feeling of betrayal and do what I came here to do. "Sloan is on his way, right?" I look to Lucas, and he nods. "Good."

Charlie tips her head. "What are you doing, Teddy?"

I want to tell her I'm finally putting an end to all the bullshit. That I'm getting to the bottom of who murdered her father in hopes she'll forgive me, but I can't bring myself to do it. I don't know if it's my pride or the fact I'm still so angry with her about everything, but I just can't.

I continue to ignore her question, the same way she practically ignored me. I try to focus my attention on Julius. "Take her upstairs and write down every detail you can remember about where Emil is holding our stuff. I have a plan."

She inhales sharply through her mouth and shakes her head. "Teddy don't do this. It won't end well."

I close my eyes for a second and smile at the fact she knows exactly what I'm planning. She's always had a way of knowing things before I say them. It's one of the many things I loved about her.

Loved…

The word bounces around my mind and almost makes me sad. An emotion I've kept under lock and key beneath my heart. An emotion I swore to never feel, but that's the thing with Charlie… She makes me feel.

For the longest time, all of the years I spent watching her, and the weeks I had her before I left, my love for Charlie was never a question. I knew I would step in front of her if war came. Take any bullet, challenge any man—I would have done anything for her. But now my mind is questioning my love for her all on its own.

I shake the thoughts away and look back to her. "I'm doing what needs to be done. Go with Julius and draw up a map for us to follow."

She pauses, her mouth slightly open like she wants to say more, but she doesn't. She disappears up the steps with Julius.

Once they're out of sight, I turn back to Lucas. I want to say something, anything, but I can't even bear to look at him the same way. Thinking about him and Charlie together makes me angry. I can feel the blood in my body boil. My heart races, ready to explode, but I don't act on it. Keeping your composure when you're in a position like mine is key. If the enemy sees your own walls crumbling, they'll light the match to speed up the process.

Cedric always told me love is a killer. I never knew what he meant, but I'm seeing it now. It kills you inside slowly at first, but you don't notice because it's masked with lust. Then, slowly, it seeps to the outside, coating every surface, space, and person within reach. The problem with that? All of my love died with Charlie. Every ounce I had to give I gave to her willingly. I let her take it, use it. I let her change me. I knew it was only a matter of time before something like this happened, so why am I so damn angry about it?

I push away the thoughts and inhale deep through my nose. If anyone is to blame here, it's Charlie. She's the outsider, not

Lucas. She's the one who wrecked what we had, and I fucking let her. But not anymore.

Before I can finally break the silence and ask some bullshit question to fill the quiet space, a knock sounds out from the other side of the door. I lock eyes with Lucas before turning and opening it.

Sloan stands on the other side in his khaki suit with his gold badge pinned above his heart. "Evening, Chief." The look on his face is one I've seen before, but instead it was Charlie who wore it.

His eyes scan over my entire body, lingering on every inch. "What the fuck," he whispers. "You're dead."

I smile. "As far as anyone knows I am. But I need your help."

He holds up his hand and shakes his head. "No. Let's go back to the dead part first. You can't die, then suddenly reappear and not expect me to ask questions."

I do my best to explain my plan as quickly as possible, telling him why I decided to fake my own death and anything else he may want to question.

"So, you did it to trick the leader of the cartel out of hiding?" He raises a brow and snorts. "How'd that work for you?"

I cross my arms over my chest. "Honestly? Pretty well. I actually have a lead to follow now. Something I wasn't able to obtain with even your help before."

The small smile falls from his mouth. "And they knew this

whole time?" He points to Lucas.

"They, as in the twins, yes. Charlie, no."

He closes his eyes as he leans his head to one side, then the other like he's stretching. "You know, before Charlie's dad died, I made him a promise to watch over her. That meant physically and mentally. If anyone tried to hurt her, I'd hurt them. And you know what you did?" He doesn't let me answer. "You hurt her, Theodore. That girl was broken."

"You don't think I know that?" I step closer to him.

"No. I don't think you do. If you actually gave two fucks about her, you wouldn't have put her through all of that."

"It was for her own good. I needed this to be believable. If she knew, I wouldn't have been able to stay away."

A sad snicker escapes his mouth. "You know how I know you don't care about her? Because if you did, it wouldn't matter if she knew or not. If you cared, you wouldn't have been able to stay away. Period. You're more in love with the idea of her than you are actually in love with *her*."

His words stop me in my tracks and vibrate through my mind. Maybe the old man is right. I brought her here on my own agenda first. Used her for any information she had on the cartel. We wanted the same result, so it was okay. But the more I think about it, the more Sloan's words settle into me.

Everything I love about Charlie had some sort of benefit for me. Her body? I'd fuck her for a release. Her personality? Fuck. She's nothing but bratty, but at the same time, she can definitely hold her own in a battle of wills. If you're going to fuck with the mafia, you need that. You need to be smart. Her being able to handle herself physically was a bonus too. I wouldn't have to watch every move she made or worry she'd end up dead because I know she wouldn't let it happen.

"Here's the stupid map. I don't see why you can't just take us there."

I look behind me and see Charlie descending the stairs as Julius follows. I don't even have time to reply to Sloan before she's next to me, shoving a piece of paper into my chest.

"We will all be going, but for now this is going with him." I take the paper from Charlie and fold it up before handing it to Sloan. "Take this and leave it on your desk or somewhere visible. I want Snyder to see it."

He levels his eyes with mine before snatching it from my hold. "We aren't done with our conversation," he says as he opens the door.

I give him a crooked smile. "We never are, Chief."

Another huff comes before he steps out and vanishes.

"What conversation?" Charlie questions behind me as I watch Sloan's taillights grow smaller and smaller.

"Don't worry about it."

I can hear the attitude and frustration in her voice. "Care to tell me why you wanted him to have that, then?"

I close the door and look back to her. "If Snyder finds it, I'm sure he'll tell the ATF agent which will result in more snooping around trying to pin down the location of what you wrote down. When that happens, I guarantee he'll come knocking on our door wanting more info. When he does, we will give him exactly what he wants."

She crosses her arms and pops out her hip. "Yeah? And what's that?"

"Someone to pin shit on. We're going to give him Emil."

CHAPTER FOURTEEN

Charlie

I pace the floor in my room, trying not to freak out over what Teddy has planned. When Chief Sloan left, I was speechless. Words refused to formulate sentences, then travel to my mouth. I wasn't completely sure what Teddy wanted to do, but I had an idea. I was just hoping I wasn't right.

My door swings open as Teddy steps inside. "Charlie, we need to talk. About last night—about today."

"There is nothing to talk about. You're an idiot and have a death sentence obviously. I thought maybe you were smarter than this, but clearly you're not." The words come out quick and sharp without even thinking, unlike a few moments ago.

He lets out a single huff, then rushes toward me.

"What, going to grab me by the throat again and tell me

how you're in charge? Or how I should watch my mouth? I'm done listening to you."

I'm not sure if it's the anger from last night or the complete bewilderment at what he's doing, but I'm not lying. I don't care anymore. And maybe that's the problem with love that comes so quickly.

You get caught up in the honeymoon phase and think that's how it'll always be. You don't take the time to learn who your partner really is. Sure, I knew Teddy was a bad guy. I just didn't think he was *that* kind of bad guy. The one that would treat me like dirt over something I've already tried to correct. Something I've already apologized for. I don't think he realizes it, but he's doing nothing more than pushing me away even further.

I turn and try to retreat to my bed, but he catches me by surprise yanking me back by my hair. His face comes over my shoulder and rests by my cheek. "You really think you run this shit, Charlotte? Because you don't. If I were smart—which I'm obviously not because I fell for you—I would kick you on your ass to the curb. Too bad I still want you. I still need you." His words are a hiss.

"You can think whatever you want if it'll make you sleep better at night. That I love you, or you're better than all of this, but it won't change the fact of who you are and what you've done. *You're—*" He kisses my cheek. "*—a—*" His lips find my jaw next. "*—whore.*" Pain vibrates through me as his teeth dig into my neck, and then he pushes me away, still holding my hair.

A silent sob claws at my throat, begging to be released,

but I won't let it. Instead, I bite my lip and prepare myself for whatever he throws at me next.

"You know, Charlie, I tried to give you everything you could ever want. You've never had to ask for a single thing. And the way you repay me is by defiance? By sleeping with someone I practically raised?"

Anger vibrates through my body. "I never slept with Lucas. Never." The words grind out between clenched teeth.

His grip on my hair tightens. "I don't believe you," he whispers. I hear the buckle of his belt coming undone followed by the low sound of his zipper. "I'd be a fool to believe such a lie."

My eyes stay glued to my bed in front of me as he lets his body lean into mine. "I don't care what you believe anymore, Teddy. Nothing I say even registers with you."

He snaps my head back, bringing his face next to mine again. "Good."

Everything that comes next happens so fast and so slow—all at once. He pushes up my dress and rips off my delicate panties. They never stood a chance against him. Normally his roughness wouldn't bother me, but this is different. He's like a completely new man doing anything he can to hurt.

"Teddy, no!" I yell, but it's no use.

"What's the matter? Don't want to fuck because I'm not Lucas? Or have you moved on to the cop now?" He laughs. "Did you think I wouldn't find out how you *talked* to him? See, from what I saw, I couldn't figure out if you were trying to get information or seduce him. Probably the latter."

My body freezes.

"Didn't think I would know about that little exchange too? Don't you know by now that I see everything."

Suddenly, my heart breaks. Literally breaks. I can feel the small threads that have been barely hanging on finally snap, sending my heart shattering into my ribs. I'm not sure if this is just the last straw, or maybe the fact I've felt too guilty to realize how terrible he's been, but nonetheless, every piece of my heart sinks to my stomach.

I grab my hair above his hand and yank myself away, then turn to face him. My voice is a murmur. "Why are you doing this? Why do you want to hurt me?" Tears fall from my eyes and hit my cheeks, but I push them away roughly with the back of my hand.

His eyes meet mine, and for a split second, the fight leaves.

His blue orbs become soft as he studies my face. "I need you to hate me, Charlie."

"Why?"

"Things are just easier when you hate me."

His confession is the light at the end of a dark, dark tunnel. It gives me hope, but it's short-lived.

Just as quickly as the fight left his eyes, it returns. With one hand he pushes me to the bed as the other finishes the job of pulling down his pants. I try to raise up—to run—to do anything other than let him on top of me, but he crawls over me, securing his palm in the center of my chest.

"Teddy, please," I beg, but it falls on deaf ears.

I claw at his arm and wiggle my way up the bed as far as I can go, but he's stronger. I try to remember everything my dad taught me, but when I see his face, I can't bring myself to jab his eyes or push my palm into his nose.

"*Teddy*!" I scream.

No response.

I look to my side for anything I can grab to try and fight him off, but he acts before me. He clasps both of my hands in one of his, then uses his other to flip me over. He lets my hands go only long enough to pull them behind my back.

I feel like a fish out of water, jerking and kicking, but with his hands around mine and his knees engaging mine, nothing I do is any use.

"Teddy, please. Don't do this," I cry.

Again, he doesn't respond.

Soft fabric loops around each of my wrists, then tightens, and everything in me goes still. My thoughts are erased. My body turns lax. And my fight completely evaporates.

"Hate me." I can feel his hot breath on the back of my neck as he pushes into me. "Please."

The pain in his voice doesn't match his actions, and it confuses me, but everything about Teddy since I've been back has confused me.

"I"—*thrust*—"need"—*thrust*—"you"—*thrust*—"to"—*thrust*—"hate me."

Pains tears through my core as screams threaten to escape

me, but I swallow them down. I won't let him know he's killing me slowly. He pulls out and I hear him spit before he dives back toward me.

He pushes his hand into the side of my face before hooking two fingers into my mouth and prying it open. Tears bite behind my eyes before they finally fall again, soaking the bed beneath me. And just when I think it's finally coming to an end, he pulls out and flips me over.

One arm drapes over my stomach heavily as the other grabs my chin and forces me to look at him. "Look at me while I do this."

I give in to his command and stare at him with cold eyes and a quivering lip. His eyes are empty. Dead. Sweat beads down the side of his face, dripping onto me, feeling like battery acid. He bares his teeth and growls as he fucks me harder and harder, breaking my soul with every thrust.

Finally, he comes with a roar inside of me. His hand releases from my chin, but he keeps his arm over my stomach, trying to gather the last bit of strength he has.

When he finally pulls out, I'm not sure what to do with myself. My mind is a complete haze, and my body feels like it's in shock. My arms are screaming to be released as the pain continues to pulsate from my shoulders all the way down to my hands.

He steps back into his pants and leaves the room like it's just another day with zero care for me.

I stay in the bed, replaying the entire ordeal over and over again in my head. What did I do wrong? Why did I deserve it?

All questions I ask myself and can't even answer. Everything I try to counteract it with is nothing more than a pitiful excuse to stick up for Teddy. Maybe he didn't mean it. It was me, I made him angry, but that's all bullshit. Teddy is a ruthless fucking criminal. A mafia leader. A murderer. Rape wouldn't be something beneath him.

I stand from the bed and wince at how sore I am from being pried open. Cum trickles down my legs, sinking into the carpet, and I'm completely disgusted. All I want to do is get Teddy off me. He touch, his smell, his fucking cum.

I rush to the bathroom with tears flowing down my face and a sob finally breaking free. I try to turn the water on, but it's no use. My hands are still bound, so I sink to the floor instead and let myself cry. I let myself really mourn because the man I loved really did die. All of the tears I've shed for that man don't even compare to now. My Teddy is gone, and a monster is in his place.

CHAPTER FIFTEEN

Lucas

BANG! BANG! BANG!

It takes me a minute to realize I'm not dreaming and that someone is actually banging on my door. It can't be Julius. He has no respect for privacy, and Carl doesn't knock like the motherfucking police, so that leaves two options. It's Charlie or Teddy.

The thought of Charlie needing me, or that something is wrong, has me bolting upright, not even bothering to wipe the sleep from my eyes. As far as Teddy…

I don't bother putting on a shirt before I sprint across the room and to my door. When I open it, the sight on the other side has me questioning a lot of things. I've worked under Teddy for the past eight years, and never once have I seen him broken.

I've seen him mad enough to burn down buildings, sad enough to scream, but never broken. Never broken and… crying. "Boss?"

I'm not sure what I'm supposed to say or do with him in front of me. Brotherly love is kind of a foreign concept. We don't hug. We don't comfort each other. And we most definitely don't fucking cry. Sure, he isn't a blubbering mess, but Boss has never been one for dramatics. If it wasn't for the light from the hallway shining directly over him—making the streaks of almost dried tears on his cheeks glisten—I wouldn't know he was crying at all.

"Lucas, I need you to go take care of Charlie." His voice is cracked and weak.

"Take care of Charlie?" I tip my head to the side. When I'm told to take care of someone, that means one of two things. Either keep them quiet or shut them up. "What do you mean?"

When he doesn't respond, I know things are bad. He's never had a problem clarifying before which only makes me more confused.

I glance to the other side of the hall to make sure it's clear before I pull him into my room and quietly close the door. "What did you do, Theodore?"

I never use his name, but something in me tells me that whatever he's done must be bad.

Finally, he looks up from the floor and meets my eyes. Pain and regret swirl in them. "I fucked up. I really fucked up."

Just the mention of Charlie accompanied with his words

make my blood boil. I told myself from the very beginning I wouldn't love her. I couldn't. She had already been claimed, and, lord have mercy, on any man who tried to cross the boss. But seeing her so distraught and shattered did nothing but make me want to help her—comfort her.

I knew doing anything with Charlie was a bad idea, but I took the plunge. When she kissed me, I didn't stop her. I needed to know what she felt like, what she tasted like. I needed to know what powers she had that made men like Teddy not even question walking to the ends of the earth.

I never had a mom, so the concept of loving a woman has always been unfamiliar, and all the women I've slept with have never caught my attention for more than a few minutes to get my dick wet.

Charlie though… There has always been something about her. The way she moves with complete and total confidence even when no one is watching. When she thinks I'm not watching. How she can hold her own in a fight and give an attitude like it's her first language. Something about her has always intrigued me, and maybe that's where I fucked up. Knowing damn well her and I would never happen, yet still letting myself dream about it.

"I hurt her, Lucas." Teddy's voice drags me out of my thoughts.

"What do you mean hurt her?" My fists ball on instinct, and my chest heaves with the rush of adrenaline.

He looks at me up and down before nodding. "Do you love her?"

His question catches me off guard. "What the fuck kind of question is that? Of course I don't. She's yours, boss. You've made it *very* clear."

A sad huff escapes him. "She's not mine anymore, so I need to hear you say it. Tell me you love her."

I squint my eyes. "Do I need to call Dr. Kelly? You're clearly losing your mind. Just tell me what you did so we can fix it."

I almost feel like a father trying to get through to his child which is weird. The roles have never been reversed like this with Teddy and me.

He sits on the edge of my bed and lets out a deep breath. "You know, when I first put the pieces together that something was happening between you and Charlie, I was mad. Utterly fuming ready to kill you. Hell, maybe I still am a little. But yesterday the chief said something, and it made me wonder. This whole time I've been trying to hurt Charlie. I thought if I pissed her off enough, she'd open up and tell the truth, but when the chief said I don't care about her, only the idea of her, it made me think maybe he's right.

"Honestly, I love her. Sure, I've questioned it a bit since I've been back, but wouldn't you?" His eyes burn into me before he looks to the floor again. "I want her to be happy, Lucas. I want her to know how loved she is. And with what I'm about to do, I don't think I'll be around to fix everything I've fucked up. I did what I did to her so she would hate me. I *need* her to hate me."

"What did you do?" I grind out through my teeth.

He stands and smiles sadly. "Go take care of your girl."

As he leaves the room, I hurry out my door behind him. He goes right and I turn left, heading straight to Charlie's room. For a split second, I almost feel like I'm being set up. Him essentially letting everything go makes no sense to me, but the sinking feeling in my stomach tells me otherwise.

I steal one last glance to my right and see the front door closing. Turning back to Charlie's door, I take a deep breath and knock. Then knock again. I knock a total of four times before I crack it open and peek inside.

"Flower?" I question out to the dark.

When I don't hear her response, I flip on the light. The scene before me has my stomach rolling and every fiber in my being on high alert. Her bed is disarray. Pillows are thrown to the floor, her duvet is pushed all the way to the left, and small bloodstains smear over her sheets.

Not seeing her there sends me into a panic mode until I step forward and see her sitting on the bathroom floor with her hands behind her back. Her dress is hiked up her legs, displaying a naked bottom half with blood and other liquid painting the inside of her thighs.

Immediately I'm caught between helping her or hunting Teddy down. I jerk my chin into the air and hit the wall next to me. Charlie jumps with the sound and moves her eyes to mine. "Please not you too, Lucas." Her lip quivers and her body shakes.

Suddenly, all of the disgust and anger leave me and become replaced with sadness. She wouldn't think I'd actually hurt her, would she? I sink to my knees and bite back every word I want to scream.

I crawl in front of her slowly. "I'm not going to hurt you, Charlie. I would never hurt you." I reach out to brush the hair from her face, but she flinches again.

"Teddy said the same thing."

I rake my hands through my hair, then drag them down my face. Right now, Charlie needs me to be soft. She needs me. I sink back to my knees and hold up my hands. "Look—" I clear my throat. "I promise I'm not going to hurt you, okay? Let's just focus on getting you cleaned up for now, and we will go from there." She looks at me with skepticism in her eyes and doesn't respond.

I reach out again, slower this time, and lightly nudge her shoulder forward to see behind her back. I unbind the red tie that's knotted firmly in place. Once the fabric is clear of her skin, red marks and indentions snake around her wrists, adding more fuel to my fire.

I move her back to her place and sit directly in front of her. I don't want to scare her or move too fast, so I'll let her go at her own pace.

After a few silent beats, she finally breaks the silence. "What did I do to deserve this, Lucas?"

The pain in her voice paired with her bloodshot eyes and shaky body have the beast in my body raging. But on the outside, I stay calm. "You didn't do anything, Flower."

She smiles with a quiver before scooting closer to me and leaning her head into my chest. "I really did love him."

I wince with her confession even though I've already known this. "I know." I pet her hair.

"I don't think I love him anymore." Her voice fractures.

"I know."

I should probably say more or do more, but I'm just not sure what. At this point, all I'm seeing is red, and I'm ready to take every ounce of it out on Teddy. So instead of talking, I do what she's used to. I comfort her the same way I've done numerous times before.

I gently push her away and stand from the floor. "I'll be right back."

If she would have asked me to stay, I would have, but she didn't object. She let me leave her room without a fight, but imagining how the scene between her and Teddy played out, I don't blame her. She's out of fight for the night.

I hurry back to my room and snatch the dark blue comforter from my bed before hurrying back to Charlie's. It's probably best Teddy has left because there is no telling what I would do if I saw him right now.

I drop the thick comforter in the bathroom doorway before walking to the sink and grabbing the washcloth next to it. I wet it with warm water, then lean back down to Charlie. "I'm just going to clean up your legs a bit, okay?" No words come from her mouth, but she nods with approval.

Lightly I brush the cloth over the inside of her thighs, making sure I don't go too high to make her uncomfortable. After I wipe away all of the blood and cum from the worthless bastard, I hand it to her and turn around so she can clean the rest of herself with a little privacy.

After a moment, I turn back around and see the cloth lying on the floor in front of her. The white terry cloth material is now stained a dark pink. I try not to focus on it, but my eyes keep finding their way back to it. I finally shake away their persistence before I pick up the comforter and wrap Charlie in it.

A groan leaves her lips as I hoist her into my arms. "I'm sorry." She nestles her head to my chest without a word.

I carry her from her bathroom, down the hall, and then into my room. I set her gently on the bed, scared I'll hurt her. I've always seen Charlie as somewhat fragile since she's a woman. Every time we would train together, I did my best to take it easy, but her strength always proved to be more than I thought. But right now? Right now Charlie is fragile. The man she loved raped her. He put her through something no woman should ever have to go through and then came to me to clean up the mess.

I've always had respect for Teddy. He's taken me and my brother in, helped raise us to be like him, but this isn't who I thought he was. Something like this is never okay, so I'll take all he's taught me and use it against him. Loyalty or not, he fucked up and he knows it.

I grab a shirt from my dresser before walking back to her. I slip it over her dress, not wanting to make her uncomfortable by undressing what little clothes she has on. "You can stay in here tonight. I'll take the floor."

I lean her body onto my pillow, then pull the comforter

back over her before settling on the floor right next to my bed.

"Lucas." A quiet cry comes from her. "Please."

Without another word, I already know what she's asking, so I get up, crawl into the bed next to her, and do what I do best when it comes to Charlie. I fall right back into our old routine and hold her while she cries.

CHAPTER SIXTEEN

Teddy

I rip off the rearview mirror as I drive away, then throw it out the window. I can't bear to even look at myself. Disgusted, ashamed, hurt. Some many emotions roll through my mind as I push this shitty Honda to its limits.

I'm not really sure where I'm going, I just know I need to be far away. Once Lucas walks into that room, which I'm sure he's done by now, I know he'll be out for blood. I would be too if the roles were reversed. I'm just glad I have someone I can count on to make sure she's okay.

The road curves over and over as I follow it. My headlights don't provide much light, but they give me enough. Enough to see the road narrow in front of me, giving me a split second to contemplate continuing with the turn or going straight off the shoulder. I punch the steering wheel as I turn it. Crashing would be a fucking cop-out.

Fucking pussy.

Finally, I slow and pull over when all the streetlights disappear and the city noise dies down. Throwing the car in park, I use my free hand to fish out my phone.

I stare at the screen for a long minute before I finally dial Julius.

The receiver clicks, indicating he's picked up, but I know he won't speak. "Go check on your brother." I hang up without a goodbye.

Stepping out of my car, I circle to the hood and plop down. "What the fuck is wrong with me?" I whisper to no one.

I love Charlie. God do I fucking love her, but knowing another man has touched her fucking kills me. I want to try and convince myself I only loved the idea of her—like the chief said—but it's a fucking lie.

Charlie isn't just an idea. She's a whole fucking novel with immaculate detail on crisp white pages penned in fresh black ink. The type of novel you read and fall in love with simply for the fact that it is such a puzzle. One whereby the end your heart is ripped out, stomped on, and shoved back into you. She isn't an idea. She's a fucking story. A story you can't forget once you're done.

I grip my hair in between my fingers and yank. "*Fuck*!"

What have I done? Never once have I been the type of person to let shit get to me or let people inside my head. This whole time I've been back, I've done nothing but hurt her over and over. I've done nothing but prove to her I am a monster.

A single tear escapes my eye and rolls down my cheek. As much as it hurts, maybe this is for the best. Charlie deserves nothing but perfect, and I'm just not it. And that—that is how I know I love her. I'm willing to push her away, make her hate me, just so she can be free of the burden of me.

CHAPTER SEVENTEEN

Charlie

My body aches in ways it never has before. My legs are sore, my arms are sore, everything is sore, and I can't stop crying. At this point, I'm pretty sure there is no water left in my body with all the tears I've shed.

I turn slowly in Lucas's hold, grimacing at the sharp pain it brings. "Hey, you okay?" His voice is groggy but still full of concern.

I nod, then realize he probably can't even see me with all of the lights off. "I'm just… sore."

Before he can reply, his bedroom door creaks open. My body goes rigid and tight like it's ready for a fight even though I know I'm in no shape to be kicking anyone's ass. A large figure stands shadowed in the doorway for a moment before they speak. "What happened?"

Comfort and ease wash over me when I realize it's only Julius. I'm not sure what it is, but I've always felt comfortable around Julius. Maybe it's because he's so quiet or because I know I have nothing to worry about when he's around, but regardless, he brings me ease.

"Julius." When his name leaves my mouth, a new wave of grief washes over me.

As much as Lucas makes me feel safe, I still worry about what Teddy will do if he found us like this. It's something I shouldn't have to worry about considering how he left me, but I can't help it.

I stand from the bed and pad to Julius slowly. When my feet stop in front of him, I look up into his eyes. I think maybe he knows I don't want to talk about anything and just need to be held because he reaches down and wraps his arms around me.

Silent dry sobs rack my body of their own accord, but he doesn't turn me away. "I'm going to take her with me."

It's always a startle to hear his voice since I don't hear it often, but something about this moment—me in his arms with my head pressed to his chest—brings me salve in the vibrations of his deep baritone.

Without speaking, I can see Lucas nod out of my peripheral, then lock his eyes with Julius. They almost mirror one another with every feature they have, but this time, Lucas wears a concerned look while Julius seems almost tranquil. More unspoken words are exchanged before Julius scoops me up and goes back into the hall, then into his room.

Where Lucas's room is dark with deep wood furniture and no color, Julius's is the total opposite. A gray platform bed sits directly in the middle while dim bulbs splash light onto almost every surface. Vintage posters of pinup girls and classical cars adorn the walls, and white bedding sits messed up and lazily on his bed and the armchair in the corner.

"You don't have to tell me what happened if you don't—"

"He raped me, Julius." The words slip out too easily.

I can see him flex his hands over and over while they hang to his sides, but his face and tone stay placid. "Okay."

He guides me toward his bathroom, but nothing else escapes his lips before he walks to his closet. When he returns, he hands me a plain T-shirt and some boxers. I take them with a shaky hand. "Lucas already gave me a shirt."

He nods. "I know, but I figured you would want him off of you. I'll wait here while you shower and call Dr. Kelly."

He turns to go back to his bed, but I catch his arm. "Please don't call him. I'm fine. I don't need him."

He inhales through his nose. "Charlie, we need to make sure you're okay."

I flash him a weak smile. "I'm as fine as I can be. Please don't make me face the embarrassment of telling someone else. Please," I beg.

He reaches up and rubs his eyes, then takes in another sharp breath. "Okay."

We stand on the threshold of the bathroom in a weird,

awkward silence. At least it's awkward for me. I'm sure he's used to it. "Will you sit with me?" I'm not sure why I ask, considering all of the events of tonight, but I do.

He nods and follows me further into the bathroom. I set the clothes on the counter as he walks to the tub, a tub much smaller than Teddy's, and starts the water.

"I won't look," he remarks as I dart my eyes around the room, gripping the bottom of the shirt Lucas gave me.

He turns his back to me and lets me undress in peace. First I slip off Lucas's shirt, sucking in his smell left lingering on it, then pull my dress down and let it bunch up around my feet. When I step in the water, it is warm and consoling. Easily I sit, then lean back, letting it circle around me.

"You can turn around." I pull my knees to my chest and wrap my arms around them.

Julius completely ignores my naked body, and I'm thankful. He grabs the detachable showerhead and starts letting the water run over my hair. I lean my head back and close my eyes. "Why do you care about me, Julius?"

I can hear the smile in his voice when he answers. "I care about you at this moment because it reminds me of a time with my mom. A little morbid, I know, but my dad was never really good to her. He did this—" He motions to my body instead of saying the word. "—and so much more. I was the one who helped her. Lucas too."

I open my eyes and turn my head as he lathers shampoo in his hands. "What happened to your dad?" I want to change the subject from myself and his mom and all the bad shit she and I seem to have in common.

"We killed him." His face never falters, and his voice stays calm like he's telling me the day of the week or some other pointless shit.

You'd think I'd be surprised, but I don't think anything could surprise me at this point. Everything just seems like some sort of fucked-up acid dream.

I try and push the thoughts away as he rinses my hair. Once he's done, he stands and grabs a towel from the wall, then opens it. I step into it, letting him wrap me up before he leaves the room.

Once I'm dry and have the clothes he gave me in place, I walk out of the bathroom feeling a little better that I'm clean. That Teddy is off me and washed down the drain with all of the dirt and grime.

Julius comes to my side and puts his arm over my shoulder to lead me out of the room. As he opens the door, he leans down and whispers in my ear. "Don't worry, Charlie. We'll protect you."

CHAPTER EIGHTEEN

Cameron

Things have been too quiet lately. Not a word from David, no info from Andrew, and the Hales haven't done shit. I know because I've been watching them for the past few days, or at least watching them as best I can while being on the clock.

"I'm gone for the night, kid." Chief Sloan tips his hat as he exits the station.

About fucking time.

I only came in early to see if he was going to say anything. I know he went to see Charlie the other night. I followed him. But of course, the old geezer is as tight-lipped as ever when it comes to that girl.

When the door closes behind him, I give it a minute and

watch him get into his car, then pull away before I walk to his desk. Flipping on the small light, I scan all of the papers scattered across the old wood. Nothing seems to stand out. Traffic write-ups, to-do lists, and even a few mug shots lie sporadically on the top, but nothing I can use.

I try to arrange all of the papers back to the same way I found them before I open the first draw and… *bingo.*

I'd know Charlie's handwriting anywhere. The way her *e*'s curl slightly on the tail, or the way her *t*'s seem to lean to the side. It's one of the first things I memorized about her. Sometimes I would pretend her dad's lunch in the fridge labeled "love you" was mine. That she took the time from her day to make me something I'd love, and did it with care, because she loved me. I know it's far from the truth, but love can be built just like anything else.

When Andrew finally finds some dirt to convict the twins, they'll be thrown in jail, and then Sebastian will handle everything else from the inside. I know Charlie will need someone to lean on, someone to be strong for her, and I'll be that person. Sure, my intention with all of this shit was never to get the girl, but it would be a crime if I didn't. I want to help David first, but there is nothing wrong with taking a little something for myself—taking Charlie because god knows I've always wanted her.

I pick up the piece of paper and study the lines and letters. It almost seems too good to be true. A whole fucking map depicting a place they clearly keep their guns. It's nothing more than a square drawn on the paper, but each little section is labeled. "Supply is sitting here behind filing cabinets."

I fish my phone from my pocket with a smile on my face and dial Andrew's number. When the line connects, I talk fast. "Come to the station. Meet me in the back this time. I have something you can use." I end the call.

Poor guy is so eager to get his normal job back he's willing to do anything for a big bust. Even if anything includes a few white lies or threats.

I flip the switch to the light off, stuff the paper into the pocket on my shirt, then walk back to the front of the station and wait by the doors. When he pulls up, I'll see him slip behind the building.

Within minutes, I see his headlights splash against the pavement before they cut off and his engine is halted. As he steps out of the car, he glances to where I stand inside. His eyes don't stay locked on me for long before he slinks behind the building. I give it a second, then step out the doors, go down the steps, and follow his path.

"You need to go see the Hales again," I say, listening to the echo my shoes against the gravel sends out.

"And why is that?" He crosses his arms over his chest and grins.

I know he doesn't think my plan will work. He was skeptical to even come down here, but he did because like I said—he wants a big bust. And what's bigger than taking down an entire gun ring?

I pull the paper from my chest pocket and hand it to him.

Slowly, with his skeptical eyes still on me, he unfolds it, then looks down. "What am I supposed to do with a drawing of a random room." He turns the paper sideways. "Is it even a room?"

I snatch it from him. "This just goes to show they're keeping their shit somewhere. Where? I don't know. They haven't led me to anywhere new when I've been watching them, and I'm sure they haven't given you shit either or you wouldn't be here right now."

He licks his lips, letting out a deep breath. "So, what do you want me to do?"

"I want you to go talk to them again. I'm sure if you say the right thing to piss them off, Charlie especially, she'll retort back with info. It may not be a huge break, but it will be something. That girl doesn't like being made to feel stupid. Just piss her off and I'm sure her mouth will turn into a river."

"A river?" He huffs.

"Just shut up and trust me. I've known her a long time."

He holds up his hands. I'll trust you this time, but if nothing comes of it, I'm resulting to doing things my way." He brushes past me heading back to his car. "Oh, and Snyder?"

I turn over my shoulder. "What?"

"I don't think the girl is very fond of you. Wouldn't be a bad idea to give up. Find pussy somewhere else." He rounds the corner of the building before I can reply.

Instantly my anger flares, but I tell myself to let it go. If Sloan knew I was working with something to bring Charlie and the Hales down, I have no doubt he'd try to retaliate, and as of now, Sloan's death isn't something I want on my hands.

When Andrew slips back into his car and turns on his lights, I flip him the bird. I can see the arrogant fuck smile from across the parking lot, but I shake it away. Soon enough, he'll be answering to me. He's a fool to think I'd let him leave after he does what I want. Nothing good ever comes from loose ends.

CHAPTER NINETEEN

Teddy

"Did he get it?" It's been three days since I sent Chief Sloan away with the paper. I've been waiting by the phone eagerly because if Cameron finds what the Chief planted, that means either he or the ATF agent will be showing up to question Charlie again. And it'll give me an excuse to go back to the house.

"Yeah." Sloan's voice is raspy on the other end. "He got it last night."

"Thanks." I hit the End button, then take off my suit jacket. I know what's coming the moment I walk in those doors.

I fish my keys from my pocket, then throw the jacket over the chair. Stepping out the door of this shitty motel, I take one last breath, then continue to my car.

The whole drive my mind is in a weird fog. I would like to think maybe one day Charlie could forgive me, or maybe the twins won't kill me, but both are doubtful. I've taught my boys to take mercy on no one even if that someone happens to be me. I just pray to whatever god will listen that maybe, just maybe, part of my training didn't stick as well as everything else.

I follow the same routine I have every other time I come back to my house.

My house…

The words in my head seem so foreign. Home doesn't feel like home. Not after being gone for weeks, not after staying away since I've been back, and not since I did what I did to Charlie.

I shake away my thoughts the best I can and pull through the gate as the guard clicks a button to open it. I take my time creeping up the drive. Part of me is *scared.* I almost laugh to myself because being scared isn't something I've felt in years. Men like me don't get scared, but I know I fucked up. And I know I have to pay for what I did.

The drive finally ends, not giving me any more time to contemplate or procrastinate, and I swear things start to move in slow motion when I see Carl lingering on the steps. I take one last deep breath and step out of my car.

The sound my shoes make along the walkway is deafening. So loud, so quiet. All at once.

"The chief called me," he says as I approach, like he can read my mind, knowing I'll ask how he knew I was coming. "They're pissed," he continues as I take the first step.

"I know." I take another step.

"I'm pissed," he adds.

"I know."

"Is that all you can say for yourself? You know? What the fuck was running through your mind, boy?" His shrill voice echoes around us, bouncing off the trees and slamming back into my ears.

I shake my head. "I love her, Carl."

His hand moves from his side quickly, the back of it connecting with my face. "Don't you dare disrespect her that way. You don't love her. Here I was, trying to make excuses for your crude behavior, thinking you were simply scared to love someone so powerful. I was wrong. You're nothing but a weak, naïve child trying to play house with someone who is clearly out of your league."

My anger almost gets the best of me, but I remember I deserve this. Anything and everything from this point on, I deserve. "I was stupid. Stupid and confused, but the best thing I've ever done was make her hate me so bad that she wouldn't want me anymore."

His face softens the slightest bit. "What are you talking about?"

"We're setting up Emil. When the ATF agent comes to ask more questions, I'll give him Emil. People like him don't care who they take down as long as they get someone. And I already know Emil will find out and come for me. If I don't end up dead, I'd be surprised. Charlie hating me just makes all of this easier. She won't hurt like she did before."

He shakes his head slowly. "Your logic is so flawed, boy. That girl loves you. That feeling doesn't go away overnight, no matter what the other person inflicts. Let's just hope you even make it to follow through with your plan."

I nod, knowing exactly what he means. I'll only get to follow through if Lucas and Julius don't kill me first. He pushes open the door and steps to the side, letting me enter alone.

Immediately Lucas emerges from his room like he's been waiting on me. He shakes his head with a grimace on his face, then backs to Julius's door, keeping his eyes on me. He taps lightly three times before Julius steps out too. I nod, already knowing what's coming. Both of them stare me down as I glide past them, all the way down the hall, to the room we only use for one thing. Less than two months ago I stood in this same, ill-lit room, glaring over Hugo Moreno, trying to get answers. But now I'll be on the receiving end of things.

I don't bother closing the door behind me because I know they're following. As soon as I hear them step in behind me, I swear the walls start closing in on us. My eyes go blurry, and my stomach turns. I've molded these men to be killers. Ruthless, unforgiving killers, and now I'm their victim.

You never expect to be destroyed by something you create. But maybe that's where some makers fail. They mold people and objects into marvelous things and beings, set them on the right track, but before they know it, those things and people are coming back for them.

The door clicks closed behind them. Now it's only a matter of time.

"You know what's going to happen, Theodore." Lucas's voice is poised in a sense. Calm, even, calculated.

"I know." I repeat the same words I said to Carl.

"You won't ever touch her again." Julius speaks this time.

Every time I've heard him speak before this I felt like a proud father, but now I'm taking on the role of a scolded child. Julius never has many words, or maybe he does but he doesn't say them, but this time, I know he's serious. He didn't ask a question or leave me room to argue. He made a statement, and I have no doubt he'll enforce it.

"She trusted you," Lucas starts again. "She loved and trusted you. Do you know how many nights I held her, trying to calm the wave of emotions tormenting her body because she missed *you*? She mourned you. She fucking mourned you!" he roars. "And you come back, thinking her and I are fucking, so you degrade her, treat her like shit, do everything in your power to hurt her because you were confused, and now *this*? You make me fucking sick."

I hear him spit, but I don't see anything until it lands by my shoes. "I fucked up, I know. I'm ready."

I turn to face them and widen my stance, keeping my arms glued to my sides, hoping to protect my ribs. I tip my chin up and close my eyes. The first hit comes from Lucas. I would like to say it isn't bad, but I'd be lying.

His fist flies into my stomach, making me double over and

lose all of the breath in my lungs. Julius is next. As I'm crouched over, he jerks his knee up hard, sending it into my nose. The crunch that vibrates through my head tells me he definitely broke it. Blood starts to ooze from my nose, coating my lips, running down my chin. When I open my mouth to breathe, the copper taste hits my tongue.

Over and over they take turns hitting me, kicking me. And I do nothing to try and defend myself. It would be pointless.

I'm not sure how long they hit me, but after what seems like hours, they finally step away. I was sure they'd kill me or do more then beat me black and blue. I sigh internally, thankful they've had their fill, but my victory is short-lived when Lucas taps the door and it opens, but only long enough for Carl to hand him his knife and a torch.

"We're going to mark you the same way you tried to mark her." I can't even tell who is talking at this point.

Maybe it's all of the adrenaline leaving my body or the fact I just can't take any more, but the world in front of me starts to get fuzzy and the noises in the room fade into a dull hum. Getting tortured when you can't see it coming is far worse than watching. With my eyes swollen and heavy, there is no opening them. Not when the hot knife touches me, not when I hear them call for Dr. Kelly, and not when I hear Charlie's screams. Everything just goes black.

CHAPTER TWENTY

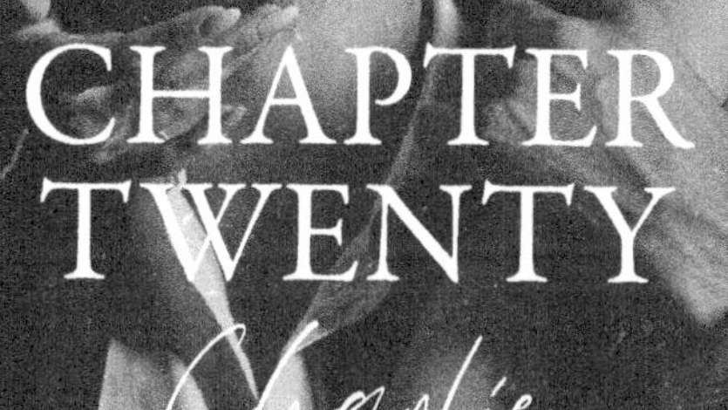

Charlie

"What did you do?" I scream as I push past Carl.

"We needed to show him what he did wasn't right." Julius speaks while Lucas, for once, remains quiet.

I ignore his comment and rush to Teddy's side. Sure, he deserves bad things, but this? This is too far. As much as I would love to relish in the fact he's in pain—exactly how I was a few days ago—I just can't. Deep down, regardless of what he did, my heart still beats for him. What a stupid fucking organ. I shouldn't love him anymore.

"Call Dr. Kelly, Carl," Lucas finally remarks.

I lift Teddy's head as Carl walks away, and the twins stand undisturbed in their spots. Blood weeps from his nose and various other wounds on his face. "Fucking hell," I whisper, doing my best to make out his features.

"Let us help," Lucas says, stepping forward.

"You've done enough. Come any closer and so help me god I will fucking kill you!"

His face falls and his shoulders slump, but he's quick to cover it up with a glower. I almost scoff because I'm angry too. Angry they hurt Teddy for hurting me. They fought for me—protected me—the way he should have. Angry because despite everything he's done, I still love him so much. Angry because I'm not sure I want to love him, but the part of my heart he harbors will always win.

I put Teddy's arm around my shoulder and hoist him up from the chair he fell into when I walked in. He's almost dead weight which makes this more difficult than I thought, but I refuse to let the twins help. I hook my arm around his waist and hold his hand that's slumped over my shoulder with my opposite one. He's barely conscious, but slowly his feet scoot across the floor one after the other.

"Charlie," Julius tries to plead.

"Back the fuck off, Jules," I hiss.

Sweat starts to slick my forehead as we make it out of the door, but I don't stop. I continue until we finally make it to the kitchen. Normally, we all crowd around the island and perch on the barstools, but I don't think he has enough energy for that. I continue practically carrying him further into the kitchen until we make it to the table on the other side.

It's the type of table you'd expect in a castle. Complete wood with ten matching chairs; four on each side with one on either end, but it's never been used. Not until now anyway. My room is only a few more feet, but I didn't think I'd make it.

"Listen, Teddy, you have to help me now, okay?" He whispers something in response, but I can't make it out. "What?" I lean closer to his swollen mouth.

"I'm sorry." His voice comes out powerless and sluggish.

I take a deep breath and push back the tears that are begging to fall. "Now isn't the time for apologies."

I ignore anything else he says as I do my best to lift him onto the table with little to no help from him. Pain radiates through my back as I lift his last leg and slide it to the middle. When I'm certain he's far enough from the edges to not fall, I dash back to my room and grab some pillows and my top bedsheet.

I make it back into the hall just in time to see Dr. Kelly walking through the front door. "Charlotte." He beams, but I don't return his smile. I rush back into the kitchen instead.

When I'm finally next to Teddy again, the severity of everything finally hits me. His face is barely recognizable; his shirt is cut open, and long burn marks go from his collarbone to his hips. His eyes are so swollen I can't even make out if they're there. I drop the pillows and sheet, then shoot my hand over my mouth to try and silence the screams.

"I can't do this," I say out loud before backing out of the doorway again.

"What happened?" Dr. Kelly asks when my back bumps into him.

If I tell him the truth, that means I have to tell him what Teddy did to me, and I just can't. "Just fix him. *Please.*" My voice comes out in a desperate sob.

He nods and walks past me. I watch for a second longer as he picks up the pillows and pushes them under Teddy's head before I walk back down the hall. Lucas and Julius aren't in the room anymore, so I keep moving until I hit the gym.

Lucas is shirtless and sweaty, hitting the punching bag like almost just killing Teddy wasn't enough, but Julius is nowhere to be seen. "Hey!" I scream.

He stops his punches and hugs the bag without facing me.

"Look at me when I speak to you, damnit!"

Slowly, Lucas finally turns around. "What?" he snaps.

"Why?" There is no need to elaborate. It's obvious what I'm talking about.

He sucks in a deep breath through his nose while biting his lip. Before he speaks, a small chuckle escapes his mouth. "Why? Because he fucking hurt you, Charlie."

My anger starts to simmer again. I don't need a voiced reminder he hurt me. My body and mind already remind me enough every day. "I could have handled it, Lucas. I'm not your mother." I regret the words the moment I say them, but it's too late to take them back.

His eyes bore into mine with rage. "Don't try to talk about things you know nothing about. And don't try and piss me off because you don't know any other way to express your own anger. He hurt you in the worst possible way, so we taught him a lesson. Why are you so fucking mad about that?"

Suddenly, my heart fissures because I already know the answer. You'd think by now the stupid thing would learn its lesson, but it hasn't. "I love him, Lucas. I hate that I love him, but I fucking love him."

He huffs. "You love him? Do you think he even loves you?"

That's a question I haven't even bothered to ask myself. "I—" I cut myself off, trying to figure out the answer. "I don't know," I finally whisper.

Lucas shakes his head. "If he loved you, he wouldn't have done what he did, Flower. Remember that." He walks past me without another word.

Is it possible to love someone and hate them all at the same time? Because that's exactly how I feel about Teddy. But maybe Lucas is right. If he loved me in the first place, he never would have hurt me.

I shake the thoughts away and raise my chin. One good thing he did teach me was to hold my head high. Yeah, he hurt me, but I won't let him know how badly. Do I love him? Sure, but I won't let him know that either. I only came here for answers, not love. I'll do exactly what I'm used to. Scream, cry, let out all of my pain behind closed doors, but when I step out, I'll be hard.

I take in a breath to compose myself, then step back into the hallway and make my way to the kitchen.

Teddy is still on the table where I left him as Dr. Kelly works over him. His face is still black and blue, but all of the bloodstains are gone. "How bad is it?" I ask, leaning against the doorjamb. I won't let my heart overpower my mind this time.

"He won't die if that's what you're asking. Surprisingly, I don't feel anything broken other than his nose. These burns—" He motions to Teddy's chest and stomach as he drapes wet gauze over it. "—will probably be the worst of his healing. They're cauterized, but I know they still hurt like hell, and his face should start looking back to normal in a week or so. He'll still be bruised, but the swelling should be down tremendously. I have him on some IV meds for now. Just some basic stuff for pain and naproxen for the swelling. I'll come check on him every day."

I nod. "Thanks, Doc. I appreciate it."

He smiles, and I return it this time as he finishes bandaging up Teddy's stomach. "Well, my job is done. Holler if you need anything, okay?"

"I will."

He nods in response, then leaves the kitchen. When I hear the front door close, I take a seat in the chair to Teddy's right and start talking. Maybe the pain meds will keep him so doped up he won't remember, or maybe he won't hear me at all, but regardless, I need to get things off my chest.

"You know," I start, acting as if he's actually listening, "when I was younger, I always told my dad when I found the man I love, I'd make him take me to the beach and we would buy a house there. Why something so basic like the beach? Because I love to swim. Did you know that?" Tears sting my eyes as I wait for an answer I know won't come.

"I love a lot of things, Teddy. I love animals, loud music, driving with the windows down…" I pause for a moment. "And I love you. I thought you would be the one to take me to the beach and buy me a home there, but I don't think I want that anymore. Not with you."

I stare at his face and try to choke out the last words. "You helped reinforce what my dad had already taught me: that I am strong. And right now, I'm choosing me over you. You hurt me, Teddy. Completely fucking broke me, and I refuse to make you believe that's okay. I'm a queen—I'm just not your queen anymore."

I stand from the chair and run from the kitchen. Maybe he isn't even listening, but saying all of those words hurt. I never expected to love Teddy, but I also never expected to lose him. Not this way.

I rush to my room and close the door. I hate this is the only place I want to come, the only place I feel is my own, even after what he did. I walk to the corner where a single pillow and blanket sit, then sink to the floor. And just like every night before, I cry myself to sleep, but this time the tears aren't just from sadness. They're from feeling a sense of liberation. A sense of freedom. Whether he knows it or not yet, I am free of Teddy, and I refuse to look back.

CHAPTER TWENTY-ONE

Teddy

I hear her feet pad against the floor as she rushes out of the room, but I don't open my eyes until I know she's behind her door. When I hear the soft latch from down the hall, I finally pry my eyes open. The white light burns, but blinking a few times helps the pain go away. At least for a moment until Lucas steps into my thin line of sight.

His dark eyes stare down on me, and I feel more vulnerable than I ever have. "Haven't you done enough?" I ask because I assume he's back to finish what he and Julius started.

He chuckles. "You deserved every minute."

I nod the most I can because he's right. I deserve this and so much more.

"I heard everything she said," he adds.

I'm a queen—I'm just not your queen anymore…

Her words reverberate in my mind, and it's like adding battery acid to all of my wounds. I try and remind myself I wanted this. I wanted her to hate me, but it's almost too much to bear. I've never let myself fall for anyone, and the moment I do, shit blows up and I ruin everything.

"I don't know what I'm doing, Luke," I say out loud, not even sure he'll listen to me.

"I don't know what you're doing either. I can't even try to process your thoughts." The anger from earlier is still evident in his voice. "Why did you do it?"

"I—I want her to be happy. If I lose this fucked-up battle with the cartel, I don't want her to hurt anymore. I don't want her to mourn me again. She deserves so much more than that."

I glance to my side as he steps away. "That's a pussy way out of shit!" he whisper shouts. "What she deserves is love from the person she loves."

His body vibrates with anger. "Lucas—" I try, but he cuts me off.

"No. Fuck you, Teddy. You took a perfectly whole woman and broke her. For what? Absolutely nothing. Your reasoning is fucking stupid, but you're right. She does deserve so much more. So much more than you," he spits.

"Promise me you'll give her that, then?" The words cut my throat as they make their way out. I never thought I'd be asking someone else to love my woman, but then again, I never expected a lot of things.

"I'm not promising you shit. I'm tired of cleaning up all the mess you make. Fix your own shit." He storms out of the kitchen.

Not long after, I hear the front door close. I want to get up and chase him. Apologize for everything I've ever put him through. Apologize for all of the shit with Charlie. Apologize for everything even if it wasn't my fault, but the machine my IV is connected to beeps, sending another dose of pain medicine into my blood stream, and I pass out.

CHAPTER TWENTY-TWO

Charlie

Two weeks later…

"You figured it out, then?" I ask Julius as we walk up the steps of the house.

The past two weeks have passed almost painfully slow. Teddy has been on the mend, Lucas is nowhere to be found, and we haven't heard a peep from the ATF agent. Because of that, I've done nothing too shady. I've made a few bank runs, checked on the supply with Emil, and told Julius to get to the bottom of the note that was left the day Teddy faked his death.

"Not exactly," he says, stopping at the top of the stairs. "But we can question the guard from that day again."

I roll my eyes. "Get him here. Maybe I can get something out of him you guys didn't."

He nods and goes to say more but is cut off by the gate at the end of the drive opening. "Expecting company?" he asks.

I tip my head to the side and study the car rolling in slowly. "Are you?" I answer his question with my own.

As the car slows to a stop in front of us, I slip my hand in my bag and grip my gun. Being caught off guard isn't something I like, so I want to be prepared. The door opens, so I calmly start to inch my gun out of my bag. When Andrew, the ATF agent, is the one to step out, I shove it back into my bag.

"I had a feeling you'd be back. What do you want this time?"

Before he can answer my question, the front door opens and Teddy steps out sluggishly.

My heart drops to my stomach. "Teddy, go inside," I hiss.

He closes the door behind him. "I'm the one who called him."

All I want to do is slap him at this point. He's the one who wanted to stay hidden. Why? I have no idea, but here he is now contradicting everything he's said, showing himself to the enemy.

Andrew takes a few steps forward. "Theodore." He tips his head. "It's nice to finally meet you."

Teddy comes to my side, his arm brushing against mine, so I step to the side, putting as much distance between us as I can. His eyes shoot to me, but he knows not to question or argue. I'm not his doormat anymore. I refuse to let him push me around.

He quickly conceals his bruised ego, then looks to Andrew. "Wish I could say the same."

I glance to Julius, who is just as confused as me. I knew we would be discussing shit with Andrew, but I figured I would handle it. Not Teddy.

"Please, come inside." Teddy steps next to Julius, giving Andrew room to move up the steps and inside.

Once he's through the door, Teddy follows, but Julius and I hang back a few feet. When they're out of earshot, I grip Julius by his arm and pull him to my level. "Watch him."

He glances to the backs of Teddy and Andrew. "I won't let him try anything stupid. He's in our house."

I nod, but Andrew isn't who I'm worried about. Teddy has been a completely different person since he's been back. I don't want him to flip his lid and do something stupid like kill this guy. I don't want to deal with the drama that will come with it, and I definitely don't want to be left to clean up the mess.

I hurry and catch up to Teddy and Andrew as they walk through the kitchen's threshold. My eyes instantly go to the table, expecting Teddy to be lying there almost lifelessly like he has been until recently, but he isn't. He's standing in front of me with yellowing bruises all over his face and a slower step to his walk instead. And once again, just like every other time I stare at him too long, I'm reminded of the monster lurking under his skin.

"So you said you have information for me," Andrew bellows, interrupting my thoughts.

Teddy perches himself on one of the barstools and nods. "I

do, but you know it won't come free."

Andrew licks his lips and crosses his arms. "What do you want to know?"

I scoff. His willingness to give up whatever we want for something he doesn't even know will be worth it is pathetic.

Teddy side-eyes me again, warning me with his eyes to keep quiet. Instead of sinking into myself and doing what he wants, I prop my hand on my hip and roll my eyes. "Cameron brought you to town, right?" Andrew nods without hesitation. "Why?"

I take over the conversation, knowing exactly what information we need and what burning questions I have alone to get to the bottom of things.

Andrew shake his finger. "I gave you something. This is give and take, not take, and take. Give me a lil' something and I'll answer."

I smile. "We know who is dealing arms and where they're keeping their supply." I'm careful not to incriminate ourselves. "Now answer."

"He has a vendetta against you Hales because of her." He points to me while talking in the direction of Teddy and Julius. "He wants me to get you boys locked up so he can steal the girl."

Teddy's face goes pale, and his hands start to shake. I inhale deep through my nose, then step next to Julius and whisper in his ear, "Get the guard. Now." He nods and walks out of the room.

If I can prove Cameron sent the note, that means not only do I have to worry when I'm around him or at the station, but now I'm not even safe in my own house.

"What else?" Teddy grinds through his teeth.

Andrew laughs. "Remember, you gotta give to—"

He's cut off when Teddy leaps from the barstool and grabs him by the front of his shirt. "We're playing by my rules. Now speak, pig."

I step in between them and pry Teddy's hands away from Andrew's shirt. "Stop," I say quietly. And just like that, the storm brewing in his eyes dies and his body relaxes.

I break my eyes from Teddy's and turn back to Andrew. "Is there anything else?"

His eyes bounce between me and Teddy for a moment before he speaks again. "He's doing all of this for his family. David, his cousin, is tangled up with the cartel, and he did something. I'm not sure what, I don't ask for many details. It makes things easier, but he said you all are getting too close, if that means anything to you."

My heart beats faster. "What does David look like?"

He quickly gives a vague description matching the man from the bank. "That's all I got. I never got a good look at him."

"I'll give you all the information you need for your sting, but we need to plan this. I need a couple of days minimum to work out some details. Got it?" I don't even acknowledge what he just said. All I'm worried about now is ending all of this. Teddy's plan is stupid, yes, but it's going to work.

"I was told I'd leave here with a sure lead," he snaps.

"You'll get more than a lead if you just shut up and do as I say," I bite back.

He shrinks under my words. "You at least have to give me a little something more."

"Emil Garcia," I state flatly, planting the seed that's soon to grow into a full-fledged garden of shit. "Now leave."

He exits the kitchen. I follow him out into the hall and watch him, making sure he walks out the door. When he's gone, I step back into the kitchen and face Teddy. "David killed my dad, and Cameron was in on it."

"We can't make assumptions until we have proof."

"I have all the proof I need, Teddy. The files, what he just said."

"Okay, but like you told him, we need a plan. I have a plan, but what's yours?"

I try and steady my nerves and relay all of the thoughts rushing through my head. "We need to get Cameron and David in the same spot before shit blows up. Maybe have Andrew meet them where Emil is keeping our supply so we can confront them, and he gets what he needs."

"Okay, but why would Andrew need them there? I'm sure they'll only come if they feel it's worth it. So we need a reason."

I run through different options in my head, but I keep coming back to the same thing. "Me. We will use me. If Cameron wants me, let's make him believe he can get me."

I can see the hurt mixed with anger swirling in Teddy's eyes, but he knows I'm right. Cameron won't care about anything unless it involves me, at least I assume with what Andrew said.

Before he can say anything else, the front door opens and

closes. Both Teddy and I walk to the hallway and see Julius standing in the foyer with a man I haven't seen before. Julius nods when my eyes bounce to his.

"We will work this out later," I whisper to Teddy before closing the distance between myself and Julius and the man. "Is this him?" I ask, stopping in front of them.

He nods again.

"I'm Charlotte. I just have a few questions about the day he died." I throw my thumb over my shoulder, pointing to Teddy.

The man's face goes pale as he studies Teddy. "I—" he chokes out.

"Don't be too alarmed, I'll explain everything later," I reassure him. "I just need to know who came through those gates that day."

He rubs his hand along his face like he's trying to wipe a nasty image from his mind. "I already told him; I only saw that cop."

"Only the cop?" I raise an eyebrow. We've already known Cameron stopped by, but the timeline of him coming here and when the note was left don't add up.

"Yeah, he came and questioned Teddy. When he came back the second time, I was confused, but he said he forgot to ask something important."

"Wait." I hold up my hand. "The second time?"

He nods slowly. "Yes. He came and left, then came and left again."

I look over my shoulder to Teddy, then back to the man.

"That's all I needed. Julius, make sure he won't be a liability about this." I point to Teddy. He nods, then exits the house again with the man in tow.

After a silent beat, I turn back to Teddy. "I know exactly how we can make this work."

He grins. "Do tell, Monkshood."

His nickname for me sends a spear through my heart, but I brush away my feelings. I'm done being sad. I'm done being angry. At this point, all I want is my vengeance, and I won't let anyone, or anything, stand in the way.

I'm not sure if he caught the split second my face relayed how hurt I was or if maybe he really didn't mean to say it, but he apologizes quickly. "I'm sorry—it just slipped out."

I ignore his statement and run down my idea as in-depth as I can.

CHAPTER TWENTY-THREE

Cameron

It's been two weeks since I gave Andrew the paper, and I still haven't heard from him. I'm getting really sick of waiting on him. I knew I would be taking a risk with him, but I'm out of options. If the Hales put together that he and I are the ones who killed Charlie's dad, I know it's only a matter of time before they come for us too.

"He hasn't said anything?" David asks, lounging on my couch.

"Nothing at all. I'll call him later and see if he's found anything yet."

"He doesn't seem like much help," he laughs. "I probably could have figured out more on my own at this point."

I shake my head with a huff. "The point is to keep you away

from everything, not dig you deeper into the hole."

"I'm not scared, cousin. I've dealt with worse than Theodore," Another laugh escapes his mouth.

"Yeah? But you've never dealt with Charlie. She's always been a determined individual, but those Hales are just putting more shit into her head. At this point I wouldn't be surprised if she'd killed someone before with how long she's been with them."

He stretches his arm across the back of my couch and crosses his ankle over his knee. "Why do you want her, then? Seems like she's damaged goods at this point."

I ponder his question before I answer. "I've known her a long time. There is just something about her. I can't explain it."

He raises an eyebrow. "Wanting this girl will probably kill you, and you can't even explain why you want her? *Cabron!*"

I take a seat next to him on the couch with a beer in my hand. "Don't call me an asshole, asshole." I smile. "Just wait. Once you see her, you'll realize why I've loved her since I was a kid. She's different than other girls."

"Not sure I want to meet the woman I screwed over. We killed her dad, remember? Pretty sure she won't be too happy about that."

"She'll understand the reasons once we tell her. She's big on family too, and soon enough, she'll be a part of our family."

He side-eyes me. "I think you're being too hopeful, cousin. If she's anything like you've said, I don't think she'll be as understanding as you think."

I play his words over and over in my mind. What if he's right? What if Charlie only sees the small picture? In reality, yes, I did this for David, but in a way I did it for her too. I know her dad wanted her to have something good. To get away from Northridge Heights and thrive. If he could see her now and know she's with the Hales, I know he wouldn't be happy. I just have to make her see everything I'm doing is to please her dad and take care of her. Sure, I helped kill him, but this will be my way to give back.

"Maybe you're right, but only time will tell. I'm almost positive I can have her eating out of my hand by the time we finish with the Hales. I just have to show her how bad they really are. That's where Andrew comes in to play. He'll help me shine a bad light on them." My words spill out with so much conviction, and at this point, I'm not sure if I'm trying to actually convince David or myself.

"Just wait," I add. "You'll see."

CHAPTER TWENTY-FOUR

Charlie

I stare at my phone screen for the hundredth time today. I've called Lucas exactly twenty-four times in the past two weeks and haven't heard anything back. I didn't think the things I said were so bad it would make him want to leave. I only spoke the truth.

I hit Dial again and bring the phone to my ear. When it rolls to his voicemail, I let out a deep breath and leave yet another message. "Lucas, I don't know what's going on with you, but I need your help. In a few days I'm going to follow through with Teddy's plan. We finally know who left the note, and I'm positive I know what happened to my dad. I don't want to say too much here, so please just come home."

I end the call and sink back into my corner with my pillow

and blanket. I've done such a good job of keeping my façade in place, but I'm tired. So fucking tired. I want to be able to let everything out and be told it'll be okay. I force my thoughts away and stand. I know I shouldn't want to, but I've had the burning urge to talk to Teddy. To feel his touch.

I throw my phone in my bag and look around the room. It just doesn't have the same feel since Teddy made the move to his room a few days ago. It is nothing more than four walls. Walls that thankfully cannot talk.

Without any more thought, I usher out of my door into the all-too-familiar hallway. It's almost as if my body is on autopilot, driven by what's left of my heart, as my feet lead me directly to his door. As I stand there, staring at the threshold, my brain applies the brakes and all of a sudden, I am frozen. My hand won't reach out to knock no matter how much I tell it to.

"You okay, kid?" The sound breaks the silence and startles me.

I glance behind me and see Carl standing in the doorway of the kitchen. His hair is tousled, and in his hand is a mug that reads *DRINK SOME COFFEE PUT ON SOME GANGSTER RAP AND HANDLE IT*. The cliché almost brings a smile to my face.

"I just…" I don't even know how to answer his question. I would like to think I'm okay even though I know I'm not. But there is just so much more to it. I abandon whatever statement I was going to say and start with a question. "Is it bad that I want to talk to him?"

He leans against the doorjamb and crosses his legs. "No. You just have to remind yourself not to let him push you around. You're a strong woman. Remember that."

"What if I'm not as strong as you think?"

He tips his head and sips his drink. "What do you mean?"

I contemplate my answer and decide to just be honest. "I love him, Carl. I know what he did was wrong, trust me, I know. But almost every second I'm not with him, he's all I can think about. I don't know how I can continue to seek feelings from someone who has inflicted so much pain on me. I know I shouldn't, that I should hate him, but I just can't. I feel what's in my heart and what's in my mind is like being stuck between a rock and hard place. A rock covered in acid and a hard place protruding with nails. I don't know what to do."

"You do what feels best for you, Charlotte."

"What if I don't even know what feels best?" My voice is meek.

"That's a battle of your own. Unfortunately, I can't help you with that, but I'll be here when you do make your decision." He winks, sips the last of his coffee, then disappears back into the kitchen.

Carl's words fuel me in a way. I raise my hand and knock one solid time, but when the door opens, all of my bravado disappears. Seeing Teddy standing in front of me shirtless, covered in healing bruises and cuts, does nothing but make me want to hold him. To tell him everything will be okay. But he doesn't deserve that from me, does he?

His eyes search my face for a moment. "Charlie?"

Hearing the concern in his voice breaks the dam inside me that's been holding all of my emotions back. I push him inside his room and slam the door as the tears start to fall to my cheeks. "Why, Teddy?"

"I didn't want to hurt you," he whispers.

I shake my head vigorously. "But you did. You hurt me so fucking bad. Why?" I yell.

The words lash from within my quivering lips and tear-streaked cheekbones. I thought I had prepared myself better. I was certain I had my feelings under control. I had worked hard on a mask that portrayed confidence and strength. I was sure it would stay in place, but as soon as that door opened, it slipped, exposing the truth in my face. I was angry again. Angry. Sad. Betrayed.

"I was preparing you, Charlie. I guess you could say, even in my darkest moment, I was still protecting you. Looking forward, if something happens to me, I thought it would be easier on you if you hated me. I wanted you to hate me."

I need you to hate me…

His words from that night echo in my mind.

"No. *No*!" My voice hardens. "You don't get to do that, Teddy. You don't get to act like the reason you broke me was for my own good. That you did the horrible things you did, because you actually do care. You don't get to make me feel things. Not anymore."

"I do care, Charlotte." His voice is lower than mine—

sincere—and it sends a spark to my chest, daring to explode and take all of what is left of my rationality with it, sending me directly into his arms. But how am I supposed to forgive him? Or even worse, what if I've already forgiven him and I just can't admit it?

Loving Teddy has been nothing less than an insane, thrill-seeking, roller-coaster ride. It's been fast and sloppy. Dangerous and addicting. So fucking bittersweet, and so fucking heartbreaking all at once. But there is no denying he is like a drug. When he's not around, he's all I want. But when he's around, I beg to be anywhere but with him. How can something be such a double-edged sword?

When he takes a step toward me, the little bit of strength I have left wavers. "Please don't," I beg.

"Don't what?"

"Don't make me fall in love with you again. It hurts right now, but I know the best thing to happen to me was losing you. We don't belong together, Teddy."

Hurt paints his face, but he doesn't push further. "You're right."

My mouth is ready for a fight before I hear his response. "I'm serio—" I cut myself off when the words finally register in my head. "What?"

"You're right, Monkshood." He steps forward again, and this time I don't stop him. "You deserve everything you want and more. It would be selfish of me to ask you to wait on me to figure out how to be all you need." He brushes his hand along the side of my face before leaning down and kissing my hair. "One day a man will come into your life and he will be all you dreamed of. He'll sweep you off your feet and head straight to the beach for that house you've always wanted. He'll be everything I can't."

He pushes past me and opens his door. The magnitude of his words finally hit me, and I realize he heard every word I said that day. That's why there was no fight, only his explanations. Suddenly, everything becomes too real. I felt decent when I was the one ending things, but now with him doing it, things are different. It is almost as if it's a whole new hurt.

My mind won't formulate any words to try and fight what he said, and there is no point. There is no going back at this point. Bridges have been burned, trust has been abolished and hearts have been broken. What's done is done, and maybe it's for the best. After all, Teddy and I were never *meant* to be together.

Happily ever afters don't exist in our world. In this world.

Still, as I search the stillness on his face for just a glimpse of emotion, I feel a certain need to argue or back track, something, but my mind won't let me. So instead, I walk past him. The hallway seems colder than before. I want to turn around, tell him I change my mind, but his door closes before I can, and it's probably for the best. I need to remember who he is. What he did. I need to do as he asked. *Hate him.*

The house seems soundless, and it puts me on edge. Or perhaps, it's always this quiet, but I've just never noticed because I've always had a distraction. I walk back to my room and sit on my bed for the first time since that night, and I don't cry or cringe. Is it possible Teddy knew exactly what he was doing? Giving me the closure I needed even though I don't feel I got closure at all.

I knead my hands over my mattress and grip the comforter. It isn't the same one I've had. It's softer and lighter, and it makes me think of Lucas. I asked him to get rid of everything, and he did, at least as much as he could.

I stand and walk to where my bag is on the floor and pick it up. I fish out my phone and see there are still no missed calls, voicemails, or texts. Granted, I was very upset after finding Lucas and Julius practically killing Teddy, but I can't think of anything I said that would warrant him leaving. Not like this—with no word. I replay the words over and over in my head, making sure I didn't overlook anything.

I thumb through my contacts. This time I stop in the *J*'s. I have tried to reach Lucas to no avail, so instead of calling him again and risking the same feeling of defeat, I text Julius.

CHARLIE: ***You still up?***

Three dots dance at the bottom of the screen before a thumbs-up emoji comes in.

I roll my eyes and laugh.

CHARLIE: ***Meet me in the kitchen?***

Again, the three dots pop up but only for a split second before I get a response.

JULIUS: ***K.***

I leave my room and go to the kitchen. When I walk in,

Julius is already sitting on a barstool with a drink in front of him. "Hey, Jules."

He turns and tips his chin. "Everything okay?"

Hearing him talk is still almost weird, but it's becoming more and more normal. At least for us.

"I talked to Teddy." I try not to let the words affect me, but they do. I feel sad, a little angry still, and somehow… relieved? I maintain composure, yet tears still bite at the back of my eyes.

He scoots the stool next to him out and gently pats the seat, motioning for me to join him. "We don't have to talk about it. Sometimes silence is the best medicine."

I nod and take a seat next to him, thankful he understands, or at least pretends to. I hate having to repeat myself and have everything play through my head over and over. I didn't come in here to talk, not really anyway; I just didn't want to be alone.

He brings his glass between us, offering me a drink, but the smell alone of the alcohol makes me want to vomit. He tips his head with a grin. "Have you eaten anything today?"

The past few weeks, my days and nights have run together, so I can't even answer that honestly. "I don't remember," I chuckle.

Without another word, he stands and walks to the other side of the bar. He pulls bread from the cabinet and starts untwisting its tie. "PB&J or grilled cheese?"

I laugh again. "Is that all you know how to make?"

He throws his hand to his chest. "I'm offended you would think such a thing. For your information, I know my way around a kitchen, but only the girls I fuck get to see that. Give them an orgasm or two, feed 'em, then send them on their way."

"You're the exact definition of a player, you know that?"

He winks at me. "You didn't answer my question, Flower."

I roll my eyes and point to the stove. "Grilled cheese."

"Coming right up."

The rest of the night, we sit in a comfortable silence while I eat and Julius drinks. Normally the quiet gets awkward, but with him it feels right. It feels safe. And in a way, it makes me feel I'm with Lucas too.

CHAPTER TWENTY-FIVE

Charlie

After leaving the kitchen last night, I found myself unable to sleep. When I was with Julius, everything was fine. His presence alone made me feel better, but once he was gone, Teddy's and my conversation came slamming back into my mind and somehow landed itself on repeat.

Even now, there is no stop or pause button. Everything just keeps playing over and over like a bad song that gets stuck in your head. I let out a deep breath and roll over to my side, hoping a change in position will help me finally get some sleep, but it's no use. It's already 8:00 a.m.

I decide to get up and just go about with my day, hoping by tonight my body will be so tired it won't have a choice but to rest. I walk to my closet and pull out some jeans and a T-shirt, then slip them on. I'm pushing my feet into my tennis shoes when I hear my phone ping.

I pick it up from my nightstand and see a text from Lucas. "Fina-fucking-ly," I whisper under my breath, but when I read the message, I don't even know what to say or think.

Lucas: ***Red Eye. RUBY RED RUM.***

I start to type out a reply, but what am I supposed to even say? I've called, left numerous voicemails, and texted even more. And now I get some cryptic-ass message that makes zero sense.

I slip my phone in my pocket before grabbing my bag and moving into the hallway. If anyone knows what this means, it'll be Julius. I walk to his door and tap it lightly.

It's only a second before he opens it and tips his head. "Everything okay, Flower?"

I pull my phone from my pocket, unlock the screen, then flash at his direction. "Do you know what this means?"

I can see the recognition on his face as he reads the five words. But he doesn't give me an explanation; instead he turns his back to me, grabs his jacket, then grips my arm and leads me to the front door.

When he opens it and tries to pull me through, I plant my feet on the marble floor and jerk from his hold. "Can you tell me what's going on? Is he okay?"

He inhales through his nose, then lets it out through his mouth before scrubbing a hand down his face. "That's our code word." He says flatly. "He only uses it for certain situations, and none of them are good, per se. I don't know why he would text you and not me."

"Code word? What situations?"

He rolls his eyes. "I'll explain in the car. Carl!" he yells behind me.

Carl appears from down the hall. Julius tips his head toward the open door. "We need to go to Red Eye."

Carl walks through the door with a nod, and then Julius follows, dragging me.

"Wait! What about Teddy?" I question. My feet stumble with the inertia of his grip, and I catch myself, taking the steps as graceful as a newborn calf.

Julius lets out a huff. "He's a big boy, Flower. He's fine." I can hear the annoyance in his voice, so I don't question anymore. He has never given me a reason to not trust him. I pull myself together and quicken my pace, allowing him to free his hold on me.

He opens the back door to the car and motions for me to slide in first as Carl enters the driver's seat. I can feel the caress of the cold leather through my jeans, and it does nothing but add to the chill running down my spine. I've tried to tell myself I don't love Lucas, and I don't, not really anyway. At least I don't think I do. My mind begs to differ, and I question my own emotions by the way my stomach is in knots and my hands are slightly shaking.

Once Julius is in place, Carl starts the car and heads down the drive. The first bit of the drive is silent, but it's an awkward silence, not like last night.

"Are you going to tell me now or let me walk into something unprepared?" I question quietly.

Julius shifts his attention from what is beyond the window to me. "Ruby red rum is what we always said when my dad was having one of his moments… we'll call them outbursts. Anyway, I can't even remember where we got it, but it's stuck all of these years."

"What do you mean outbursts?"

He shakes his head. "Don't worry about it." He looks back out the window "I just don't understand why he texted you and not me. That's something we only use if we need one another. Not necessarily trouble, but it's never been used in a good way."

"I've been asking myself the same thing," I quip.

"Maybe it's because he loves you," he whispers almost too low for me to hear.

"What did you say?"

"You heard me, Charlie." He doesn't look back in my direction, and I don't dare say anything else. This isn't a conversation I want to have right now.

I chew my lip and wring my hands the rest of the way until we're finally pulling up to Red Eye. We step out, and everything almost feels foreign. It hasn't been too long since I've been here, but it's been long enough. I do my best to stay away because all I can picture when I'm here is Simon's head painting the floor.

I shake the thoughts away and follow Julius through the door. The bald bouncer, I swear, is here every time I come, and he always greets me with the same crooked smile. "Morning,

Mrs. Hale."

I return the favor as I head through the door. It's almost like when Teddy died—everyone learned my name and knew I was taking his spot, but now that he's back—now after everything—being called Mrs. Hale makes me sick. But I don't correct him. I just stick with the smile and a nod of the head and continue following Julius.

Luckily, since it's so early in the morning, no one is really here other than a few people cleaning the floors and a bartender stacking bottles. I'm sure it takes a good amount of preparation to get ready for nights in this place. We make it to the bottom of the stairs that lead up to the most private area of the club, and there is another bouncer standing guard.

He tips his head and studies Julius before he glances up the steps. "You're new, huh?" Julius asks.

The man nods.

"He's my twin brother—you're not seeing a ghost. Now move." His voice leaves no room for an argument.

The man steps to the side meekly and lets Julius walk up the stairs with me in tow. When we make it to the top, I shake out my nerves and take another deep breath. I'm not sure what I'm supposed to expect, and I don't like that.

When Julius pushes open the door, all I see is Lucas sitting on the couch with his arms stretched out across the back and his legs spread with… Before I can register what is happening, Julius breaks up the moment with a tone I don't believe I have heard before. "Seriously?" he yells. "This isn't a fucking emergency."

It isn't like him to raise his voice. The woman between his knees looks up, takes a breath, and wipes the smudged lipstick from her chin.

Lucas's head leans to the side as he smiles. "Charlie. I didn't know you were coming."

When I hear his words slur, I glance toward Julius. "He's drunk."

"No shit," he bites back, full of sarcasm.

I roll my eyes and step to the side with crossed arms. Julius can handle this.

When the woman stands, I recognize her face from Emil's casino. She's the one who was all over Lucas. I'm not jealous by any means, I'm just frustrated. I didn't sleep at all, and now I'm having to help rescue Lucas from what? A bad blow job from a two-bit whore?

Julius steps closer. "Zip him up," he demands looking at the girl before he plops down next to Lucas. "What are you doing, Luke?"

"Drinking everything away. I'm tired of feeling shit."

Julius shakes his head. "You know what happens when you go on a bender. It's never good. You should have just texted me. She doesn't need to see you like this."

"Jade?" He looks between his legs where the woman is now standing. "She doesn't care." He snorts.

"No. Charlie."

Lucas looks back to where I stand. First, it's like he doesn't remember I was here. Confusion laces his features before the embarrassment sets in. "Why'd you bring her?"

"You texted her. You know damn well I couldn't shake her if she knew."

"Actually," the slut chirps, "I texted. He was rambling about Charlie and ruby red rum. I didn't know Charlie was her." Her lip curls when she says *her*, and she locks eyes with me almost as if she's looking for a challenge. Before I can respond, I hear Julius scold her.

"Fuck off, Jade. You know who the fuck she is. Now leave." Julius uses his booming voice this time, and it makes me almost jump.

She huffs, then walks out of the room, giving me a final scoff.

Once she's gone, Julius hooks his arm around Lucas's waist, pulls Lucas's hand over his shoulder, and lifts him up. "Come on. Time to go home and detox this shit out of your system."

I follow closely behind as Julius practically carries Lucas down the narrow stairs, hoping he doesn't lose his balance in the process.

When we make it to the car, Carl is waiting by the back door. "Again?" he asks.

"Again? This has happened before?" Both Carl and Julius ignore me as they stuff Lucas into the back seat.

I walk to the other side and slide across the seat as Carl and Julius get into the front. Lucas reeks of booze and bad decisions. I can smell the perfume from other women all over him mixed with the incense of a very pungent alcohol. When the car starts and we're finally moving, his limp body slumps to the side, sending his head straight into my lap.

"I've missed you." The words slip out, almost heartfelt. I'm not sure if I was expecting him to be a playful drunk, or maybe an angry one, but nothing about him says either. His tone is completely serious as his brown eyes burn into mine.

"I've missed you too, pretty boy." I'd much rather scold him—tell him how worried I've been, but what's the point. It's not like he'll remember this conversation tomorrow.

He turns his head to face my stomach and closes his eyes. I'm glad he's not looking at me anymore because it does nothing but remind me of the feelings I have for him. I'm not even sure what those feelings are, but I know they're there. I comb my fingers through his soft dark hair and study his face. Of course, I've seen Lucas and Julius numerous times, but I've never gotten the chance to *really* look at them.

His tan skin makes mine seem paler in comparison, and his dark hair almost shines a blue hue when the streetlights hit it. His tattoos paint a picture, allowing a glimpse into who he really is. Perhaps even the difficult life that has landed him in this position. I run my fingertips from his temple down to his jaw, mesmerized by the calm and relaxed state he's in. How anyone can seem so peaceful with all that's going on is beyond me.

My concentration is interrupted when we pull up to the gate. Just like every other time, there are no words exchanged. Just a simple nod and we're let in. When we make it to the end of the drive, I look out the window and see Teddy standing in the doorway. Internally, I'm already mortified. Since he's been back, I've made it a mission to stay away from Lucas, and now here I am, fondling his hair as he sleeps in my lap. It's not like it matters anymore. Teddy and I have gone our separate ways, but in a sense, I'm still scared.

When he glides down the steps and opens the back door, his body freezes for a moment. First, he looks to Lucas, then runs his eyes up to mine. "Bender?"

I don't even have time to reply before Julius is getting out of the front and coming to the back. "It's worse than last time."

I tip my head at his answer. *So this has happened before.* I want to remark, but I don't. It's clear they don't want to tell me.

Teddy nods, then sidesteps. Julius grabs Lucas and hoists him out of the car. Lucas opens his eyes, looks around, then pushes Julius away. "I'm fine."

Julius tries to interject. "No you're not. Let me help you."

When Lucas pushes him away again, he glances back to me with almost pleading eyes. "Lucas," I say, getting out and rounding the car. "How about I help you?"

He looks to me with a huff. "You're the last person I want help from." The venom in his tone has my stomach in knots, but I brush it off and keep my calm mask in place.

"Well, that's too fucking bad. Come on." I grab his arm and haul him inside, leaving the rest of the boys on their own.

I lead him down the hall until we reach his door. He slouches into the wall, staring at me as I open it. "What are you gonna do?" he questions. "Bathe me, clothe me. Nurse me back to health like some sick fucking puppy?"

I push open the door and look to him. "What's your deal, Lucas? Why so much fucking hostility. I haven't done anything to you."

He laughs, then stumbles into his room, so I follow and close the door. "I can't read you, Flower. It's like one minute you want me, then the next you don't. And then I risk everything to try and protect you and you get mad at me. You know Teddy came to me that night and asked me to clean up the fucking mess he made? You know how upset that made me? Because I knew if I would have done what he asked, you would be right back with him.

"I contemplated doing it too. Even after what he did, I still contemplated it because I know my loyalty lies with him. But I question everything when I'm around you, or thinking about you, Charlie. I ask if the sky is really blue, is ice really cold, and if I'm really willing to break my loyalty for someone who has held it longer than you'll even look my way. You make me feel shit I shouldn't feel."

I push my back against the door and try to catch the breath that's leaving my lungs. "Lucas—"

He stalks toward me, cutting me off. "Tell me to stop, Charlie. Tell me to fucking stop because I don't think I can unless you say it."

Every thought in my mind fleets along with all of the previous words he spoke. I can't tell him to stop because I don't even know if I want him to stop. His mouth is on mine before

I can blink. His lips are soft, but his kiss is punishing. He moves his hands to my hips and grips them hard, pulling me as close as I can get before we run out of space. His tongue flicks over my own and sets every nerve in my body on fire.

But then reality sets in, and the taste of the liquor on his lips makes me push him away. "We can't, Lucas."

He cocks his head to the side and looks at me with bloodshot eyes. "Why are you so scared, Charlie? Why won't you let me show you how love is supposed to be."

His question rocks me to my core, and the realization of everything that's happened over the past couple of weeks hits me, along with something else. "I love—"

Lucas cuts me off again. "Him. You love him."

"And I love you too." The words slip out before I can stop them or even think about them.

He rubs his hands over his face, then tugs his hair. "Stop, Charlie. Just stop."

"What do you want from me, Lucas? Just tell me what you want!"

"I want you! How are you so fucking blind!"

His confession makes my knees wobble and my heart beat faster. As much as I want to give in, to show him I want him too, I just can't. "This isn't right."

"Nothing in this fucked-up world is right. Why should we have to be?" His shoulders slump, and his voice starts to crack. "I want you, Charlie. Only you."

Tears form in my eyes, but I do my best to keep them at

bay. "We can't."

He nods, tipping his head so he can look at me down the bridge of his nose. "So that's it? Why'd you even come to the club, then?"

"I came because I care, Lucas."

"No." He shakes his head. "You came back to me because he didn't want you anymore."

"That isn't—"

"Leave, Charlie. I'm far too drunk to deal with this shit. It was my mistake to even say anything."

"Lucas," I plea.

"Leave!" he booms.

I stare at him for a beat, finally letting the tears fall. Lucas has always been like a volatile storm. Fine one second, completely unhinged the next. When he feels, he feels hard, and when he hurts, he hurts harder. It's one of the reasons I vowed to keep my feelings for him under lock and key. I didn't want to wake the savage within him, and I didn't want to break his heart.

I leave his room and go to my own, promising myself to never get into another situation like this.

CHAPTER TWENTY-SIX

Teddy

"I need you to take me to the airstrip, Carl," I murmur when Charlie disappears inside with Lucas.

I'd like to say I'm not affected seeing her with him, but I am. I always will be, but it's time to be the bigger man. To show her just how much I love her by letting her go.

"For?" he questions, looking to Julius for approval.

I grind my teeth. "I am the boss, Carl. Don't ask questions. I'll explain in due time."

Julius shrugs and walks inside like he couldn't give a fuck less, and I know he couldn't. The respect my boys had for me flew out the window two weeks ago when I did what I did to Charlie. It doesn't matter what excuse I give—like there is one—or what explanation I try to tell them, they don't see it. And I can't blame them. If the roles were reversed, I'd be acting the same way. It's one of the reasons I'm going to cut all my ties.

Carl re-enters the driver's seat, so I slide into the back seat. Luckily, the drive to the airstrip isn't long, but it still gives me too much quiet time. All I've been able to do for weeks is think. Normally, that wouldn't seem like such a bad thing. But when you've done something you know you shouldn't have, lost the love of your life, and are about to hand over everything else of value, it becomes too fucking much.

Carl didn't say a word the entire drive, and he doesn't say a single word when I exit. Again, I'm not surprised. I like to look at Carl as a father figure of sorts. He's levelheaded, will call your bluff, and most importantly, make sure everything you do is right in some sort of way. At this point, I've hurt him too. He thought he knew me better—help mold me into better—and hell, I did too.

As I make my way to the hangar, Carl slowly pulls away. Joseph steps out and eyes me up and down for a quick second. "Mr. Hale?" The surprise in his voice is evident.

I had forgotten almost everyone still thinks I'm dead. It's easy to forget, to get wrapped up in my own world, especially with everything else going on.

"Joseph!" I pull him into a hug. "I can't explain now, but yes it's really me," I laugh. "I need to make a trip to Mexico. Can you take me?"

Joseph never says no. I'm not sure if it's because he really does like me, or because I keep him on retainer. I give him enough money monthly to support him and his grandmother tenfold.

He looks me up and down again with a grin. "I don't get paid to ask questions, so I'll only ask one."

I raise a brow at him.

"Does your wife know you're back? Is she okay?"

I had forgot I introduced Charlie as my wife to him. I chuckle, trying to conceal my hurt, then answer. "That was actually two questions, but yes. She knows I'm back, and she's okay."

He nods. "Good. She seems like a good woman, Hale. You have to keep her around." He winks with a smile as he walks back inside to open the doors.

If only he knew how royally I had already fucked up.

The bumpy landing has me inhaling a sharp breath. Dr. Kelly said nothing was broken, but fuck if it doesn't feel like it when I'm being bounced around.

I nod to Joseph as I exit the plane. I take the narrow steps slowly, making sure I don't fall headfirst. I'm still on a cocktail of medicine, but I refuse to let anyone see me partake. I can't let them know how weak I really am.

I slide into the back of the waiting car and rattle off Omar's address quickly in broken Spanish. The man nods and takes off. When I pull up, I debate on how to go about this whole thing. I can be honest, or I could throw in a few white lies. Really, it doesn't matter which route I take. The result will be the same.

I step out of the car and walk across the dirt drive until I'm directly in front of his door. I bang the metal knocker and wait. Within seconds, the same old woman who always greets me opens the door.

Her eyes grow wide for a split second when they catch mine. "*Fantasma*," she whispers. *Ghost.* I may not be able to speak the language clearly, but I do understand it.

I give her a soft smile, trying to portray I mean no harm with the expression.

She hurries away, then returns, mumbling to Omar. When he catches sight of me, he doesn't seem surprised at all. "Hale." He nods, sweeping his arm in front of him, inviting me in. "I knew you'd be back."

I walk inside and wait for him to close the door. As he leads me to the living room, I finally ask, "How'd you know?"

He takes a seat, and I do the same across form him. "What, that you weren't dead?"

I nod.

"Let's just say you aren't as smart as you think. I know someone everywhere." His confession doesn't surprise me. I already knew this about him, but I was careful.

"Now, I wasn't positive because I never believe anything I don't see myself, but there is no question now. So, tell me why you're here. I don't suspect it's for more supply. Your wife hasn't been pushing as much with you 'gone.'" He does air quotations with his fingers.

"I know she hasn't. We've been going through our back supply first. I'm only here to give you a heads-up."

"Oh?" He tips his head and rubs his chin.

"I'm stepping away, Omar. I'm signing everything over to the twins today. I just figured I owed it to you to let you know face-to-face."

He squints his eyes. "If this is another stunt, you can save it. I don't like games, Hale."

I hold up my hands and let out a breath. "No games. I've just realized they're better equipped to handle things at this point. I have some unfinished business I'll be taking care of, then I'm out. I've done some shit I can't come back from."

He laughs. "You think it's that easy to just walk away from this life? I have no power over you, but you and I know damn well there is only one easy way out."

He levels his eyes with mine like he's trying to read my mind, but he doesn't need to. He knows I understand what he's saying. "I know."

He shrugs. "Well, I wish you the best of luck. And I didn't need the heads-up—I would have known the moment shit goes down." He winks.

I scoff and stand. "Consider it a respect thing, Omar."

"You know the way out, Hale. I'll expect a visit from your twins soon?" He posesit as a question, not a statement.

Now I shrug. "I guess you'll just have to wait and see, but then again, you'll know when it happens, huh?"

"Touché, my friend."

I shake my head and show myself out. Omar isn't a friend. Never has been and never will be, but in this business, you have to keep the enemies close.

I sink back into the car and head back to the airstrip. Another short flight later, more pointless small talk with Joseph, and I'm finally back home.

I dial Carl as we land and let him know to meet me exactly where he dropped me off. When I exit the plane this time, I roam around the small airstrip. Obviously, there isn't much here, but the beauty of the nature surrounding it never ceases to amaze me.

After a few minutes, Carl pulls up. Instead of gliding into the back seat, I open the passenger door and plop in the seat next to him.

"Now we need to hit the bank and then Red Eye."

He side-eyes me as he puts the car into drive. "What are you doing, kid?"

I glance out the window, not wanting to look into his eyes. "Something I should have done a long time ago."

I can hear the tsk in his voice when he responds. "You realize everyone will eventually simmer down. I won't say forget, because we won't forget, but things will settle down soon enough."

I know he's right, but that doesn't change things when it comes to the issue at hand. I promised Charlie something. I've gone about fulfilling that promise in the most fucked-up way possible, so it's time to just end it. Give her what she wants and stop dragging her along on a short leash.

"I know."

He sighs. "Just don't do anything stupid, you hear me?"

There are the fatherly words I was expecting. I chuckle. "I won't, Carl."

"I'm serious, Theodore. You already fucked up enough shit once. Don't do it again."

He slows to a stop in front of the bank. I step out, then look down into the car before closing the door. "I don't plan on it." I walk away before he can reply.

I walk up the steps and push through the glass doors. I don't waste any time and hurry back to Eden's office. When I walk in, she's with another client, but I don't care. I need to get all of this shit done today.

Her head raises, and confusion and shock coat her face. "Theodore?" she whispers almost to herself. It only takes her a split second to realize this is reality and not a dream. She stands from her desk and excuses herself from the client in front of her.

She circles her desk and grabs my bicep lightly, leading me to a bare office across from hers. "Excuse my language, but what the fuck?"

I try not to laugh when the wrinkles around her eyes bunch up even more with her words. "I should have called, but I'm on a time crunch. I need you to do something."

She licks her lips and nods her head quickly like she's trying to erase the shock. "What do you need?"

"All of my accounts, I need them transferred to my boys."

She places her hand on her chest. "Did something happen with Charlie?"

"No, she's fine. I just feel the boys are more equipped and prepared to handle things if they need to. Charlie wasn't cut out for this life. She shouldn't have to keep breaking her back to make sure things are straight."

She wags her finger in my face. "Now, I can see what you're trying to do. It's admirable, I'll give you that. But when it comes to love, us women are more capable then you think. It doesn't matter what we're cut out for. We adapt and overcome. She's a strong girl. She's been running things pretty smoothly in your absence. Is this something she asked you to do?"

I shake my head. "You're right, but when you don't love someone anymore, you shouldn't be left doing something because you feel obligated."

"What did you do, Theodore?" She crosses her arms over her chest.

"Bad things. Unforgivable things. I'm setting her free, Eden. Relinquishing all of her obligations to the Hale name. Trust me, it's the right thing to do."

She lets out a deep breath, then leaves the room with a shake of her head.

I can see the disappointment in her eyes as she leaves, and it pains me. Maybe I'm going soft, or maybe it's the fact I'm just growing and noticing all of the shit I never did before. But whatever it is, I don't like it. I wasn't made king by being soft or giving a fuck about anyone other than myself and my family, but things have shifted since Charlie's been around. What a fucking cliché it is to say, but she changed me. I'm just not sure if that's a good or bad thing at this point.

When Eden comes back, she has a stack of papers. "This removes Charlie from everything and grants it all to the twins. I've gone ahead and forged her signature along with theirs since it's clear they don't know about this. Sign all of the highlighted parts."

I nod and thank her with a tight smile before scratching my name in every spot she indicated. "Is that it?"

"That's it."

"Thank you, Eden. I really appreciate everything you've done for me. I can never thank you enough."

She tilts her head. "That almost sounds like a goodbye."

I smile and pull her in for a quick hug. "Maybe it is." I release her and shrug, then hurry out of the bank before anyone can see me.

"Now to Red Eye?" Carl asks as I close the door.

I nod and let him drive in silence.

CHAPTER TWENTY-SEVEN

Teddy

After we left Red Eye, I made Carl bring me home. All of the decisions I made weren't made lightly. I've taken time and thought about everything. Weighed the pros and cons, questioned everything I could think of, and in the end, this is the only thing that makes sense to me.

I always swore I would never be the type of person to fall in love and lose myself, but that's exactly what I've done. I fell for Charlie and lost sight of everything other than my own lust. She makes me feel things I've never felt. She makes me have remorse for things I've never even thought twice about. Being in this world as long as I have, I forgot that people like Charlie still exist. Sure, she's strong and passionate, ready to handle things by whatever means necessary, but she's also delicate, fragile.

Maybe that's what made me so crazy about her. She was an enigma in my world. Something completely new and foreign. Instead of taking her and learning how to love her, I tried to shove her into my own box of how I wanted her to be. I fucked up.

I walk through the door and shout for the twins and Charlie. Julius comes from the kitchen with Charlie following as Lucas stumbles out of his room.

"Where have you been?" she questions, but not in the caring way I'm used to. It's more of an annoyed scold.

"I had some business to handle. We need to talk." I glance to the boys, then over my shoulder to Carl. "All of us."

Julius walks to Lucas's side and wraps an arm around his waist. "I'm sober enough to walk. It's just the hangover is starting. Have you ever had a hangover at…" Lucas trails off, looking around at the walls before he grabs Julius's hand and reads his watch. "5:00 p.m.? It fucking sucks."

Charlie shakes her head, then looks back to me. "Well, talk," she demands.

I'm used to seeing her be this confident, hard, sassy person with other people, but not with me. It's something new that only started about a week ago. I guess when she noticed I was healing up, she just didn't feel the need to sugarcoat herself around me anymore.

I jerk my head toward the stairs and urge them all to follow as I go up them and into my office. When I sit down behind my desk, Charlie grabs the seat in front of me to my left, while

Lucas takes the right, and Carl and Julius stand behind them.

"I made arrangements today," I state.

Lucas huffs. "What, for another fake death?"

As much as I'd like to snap at him, I just can't. I'm fucking exhausted being the boss all the time. "No. I'm stepping away. Everything I have is now yours, boys. I'm done."

Julius cocks his head as he grips the back of Charlie's chair. "What do you mean, done?"

"Just done. I've come to realize you all have a better grasp on things than me. I don't have your trust; I don't have you respect. It's only a matter of time before you leave. I refuse to bring in anyone else. Trust isn't built in days; it takes fucking years. So, instead of waiting for the inevitable, I'm taking myself out of the equation."

Julius laughs. "You say you don't have our trust or respect like we're the ones who fucked it up. Don't try and put that fucking blame on us. You did it."

"Nah," Lucas chimes in. "This isn't about that at all. He's running like a scared bitch because the ATF is on us."

I lean across the desk and hover an inch from Lucas's face. "I'm no bitch, boy. Don't think because I'm stepping away means I won't beat your ass. I'm doing what is best for this family—for the Hale fucking name."

He licks his teeth and moves in even closer. "Whatever you say, *boss*."

Every ounce of emotion I've held in for the past few weeks comes rushing out. I crawl onto my desk and grab Lucas by the throat. Every noise and scream turns to muffled background noise as I watch his smiling face go blue.

It isn't until I feel cool metal on my temple that I stop.

"Get your fucking hands off of him."

I release my hands slowly and pull away from Lucas as he coughs and gasps for air. I turn to my side and see Charlie holding the gun I got her, pointed directly at me. "You wouldn't shoot me." I'm not sure if it's more of a question or a statement with how it comes out.

She moves it quickly and points it to the ceiling before firing a single shot. Every single one of us in the room jump but her.

"Now that I have your attention," she declares. "I have zero qualms about shit anymore. You wanted a fucking queen? You got one, and my only goal is vengeance. I'm sick of the dick-measuring contests, the fights, all of the bullshit. From now on, we do shit my way and my way only."

Everyone stands stock-still and stares at her.

"The only reason I agreed to get tangled up in this fucked-up mess was to figure out who killed my dad. I still don't have those answers because I've done nothing but listen to all of you. I've kept my cool, I've waited, but I'm done."

"'Bout time you put your foot down, Charlotte," Carl chirps from the back.

She glances to him and rolls her eyes. "Do you think I like acting this way? I'm doing nothing but reflecting exactly how all of you egotistical assholes have been acting. It's time to shut up, sit down, and come up with a plan. While all of you wanted to argue, I actually thought of something."

"Enlighten us, then," I reply, stepping further back from my desk.

She ignores all of us and pulls her phone from her back pocket. Her fingers rush across the screen, dialing a number that isn't saved. When she hits the green button, she brings it to her ear.

CHAPTER TWENTY-EIGHT

Cameron

I pace in front of the white fence waiting for David. He called and told me to meet him at Sebastian's which is weird. We never meet with him together. Hell, I never meet with him period unless it's important. I don't like planes either, so the short flight here is always nerve-racking.

When the black car pulls up, I suck in a breath. Sebastian knows how much David means to me, so I know it's only a matter of time before they use it against me. But when David steps out, a flood of relief washes over me.

"Fuck, David. I didn't think you were coming." I pull him into a quick hug, then release him.

He tilts his head to the side. "You know I wouldn't call unless it was important. What'd you think, he was using me to get to you?" He laughs. "Sebastian has bigger fish to fry, cousin."

I try not to roll my eyes. David knows me too well. "So, what's going on?"

He shuffles through the open gate and up the steps. "I'm not sure, but we're about to find out."

He knocks on the door, and we wait. You'd think if someone is expecting company, they'd be quicker, but not Sebastian. He enjoys feeding off fear. I'd like to say I'm not scared of him, but that'd be a lie. The man has connections everywhere and can have anyone wiped from the earth with a simple phone call.

Eventually, the door opens and Sebastian steps outside with an envelope in his hand. He never does business inside, not with me anyway.

"Boss." David dips his head and steps to the side, letting Sebastian step further out and close the door.

"What's going on?" I ask. I'm tired of feeling on edge. I want to know what's going on.

"That's what I want to ask you." His lip curls with a sneer. "I got a call from Omar and learned some pretty disturbing news."

I glance to David and raise a brow. Everyone who runs around in these illegal circles knows who Omar is. He's a man who seems to know something about everyone. And he loves using that to his advantage. Nothing is too small in his eyes to be considered ammo.

"What are you talking about?"

Sebastian levels his eyes with mine and stays silent for a moment before opening the envelope and pulling out a few pictures, then hands them to me. I take them, glancing to David. When I look down, I can automatically tell they are from some sort of security camera footage. At first, I can't see the man's face, only his back, but when I flip to the next picture, his face is as clear as day.

Blue eyes burn into me off the paper. "Where did you get these?"

Sebastian looks at me through squinted eyes almost like he's trying to gauge my surprise. "Those were taken today. Theodore Hale isn't dead."

My mouth goes dry, and my hands start to shake. Teddy is supposed to be dead. I thought I could handle the twins just because they give off a vibe that screams easily persuaded, but with Teddy back, this causes a problem.

"Did you know he was back?" Sebastian asks, dragging me from my thoughts.

"Of course not." I bounce my eyes between Sebastian and David. Their faces and expressions mirror each other. They don't believe me. "Do you think I'd be stupid enough to do this shit if he was still alive?"

Sebastian looks to David, ignoring my question. For a moment they just stare at each other and no words are exchanged, but it seems David knows exactly what Sebastian is trying to say with his eyes.

"I want this handled and handled quickly. This isn't

something I should have to worry about."

David nods. "I got it boss." He snatches the pictures from me and shoves them back into the envelope, then hands it back to Sebastian.

As Sebastian goes inside, David looks to me. "Did you know?"

"Of course I didn't. Finding out Theodore Hale was dead was just as much a relief to me as it was you."

He stares at me for a moment like he's waiting for my answer to change. But it won't.

"If I find out you're lying to me, I'll kill the girl."

Heat starts to form in my chest, then melts to all of my limbs. "If you touch her, I will kill you."

He smiles, showing me all of his teeth. "You're too deep in this, cousin. If you want to make sure everything stays hidden and get away clean, you'll forget about the girl. She's a liability."

I scrape my teeth across my tongue, trying to do my best not to explode. "She isn't a fucking liability. You'll see."

He shakes his head with a huff and starts down the steps. "Yeah, I will, huh?"

I close my eyes and take a deep breath before following him. Once we make it out the gate, my phone starts ringing in my pocket. I fish it out and look at the screen.

"David!" I grab his arm, halting him from continuing to the car. "Wait."

I flash the screen in his direction, letting him see Charlie's name dance across the screen. "Well, answer it."

I click the green button on the screen, then turn it on speakerphone. “Hello?”

“Cameron. We need to talk.” Hearing her voice right now is like a cold drink on a summer day. So fucking refreshing.

“What’s going on? Are you okay?” I glance to David and see him nod in approval before mouthing “play it cool.”

“I am for now, but I don’t feel I will be much longer. I didn’t know who else to call, but I need help.”

“Is it him?” I hiss the question through my teeth.

I hear her sigh before she answers. “So you know he’s back?”

I grin. “I had a feeling,” I lie. “Tell me what’s going on.”

“He has the ATF agent on his side now. He wants me to help with setting up Emil so it gets him off his back. I’m scared, Cameron, but he’ll kill me if I don’t do as he asks. This whole time I thought I’d be getting answers to questions I had, but I haven’t gotten anything. I want out.”

Hearing how Andrew is now conspiring with Teddy doesn’t surprise me. He always was a sneaky bastard, but everything else she’s saying worries me.

“You should have called sooner. Tell me what you need me to do and I’ll do it. I’ll get you out of this, Charlie.”

I almost forgot David was listening until he nudges my arm. He gives me a warning look, but I ignore it. I knew this day would come, and I’m not going to let it pass me by. Charlie was always meant to be mine.

“I have a plan, but I have to be careful. If he finds out I’m talking to you…" She trails off, and I swear I can hear a soft sob. "Just give me a couple of weeks, okay? I'll text you an address. Promise you'll meet me there when I say no matter what."

"I promise."

Before I can add anything else, she's already talking in a hushed whisper. "I have to go. Just remember when I text, you come. We have to be very precise with the timing, okay?"

"I got it, Charlie. Don't—" The call disconnects before I can finish.

I exhale a breath, then shove my phone back into my pocket.

"She sounded scared," David remarks.

"I know. And if she's scared, it has to be bad. She isn't easily spooked by things."

"Maybe you were right. Maybe she's exactly who you think."

I side-eye him as we slide into the car. "She is."

He doesn't dare say another word, and I'm glad. At this point, after being blindsided by Sebastian, the argument with David, and now worrying about Charlie, I'm a ticking fucking time bomb ready to explode.

CHAPTER TWENTY-NINE

Charlie

I hang up the phone with Cameron and slip it back into my pocket. "Now call Sloan." I look to Julius.

He just stares at me with a blank expression.

"Did I fucking stutter? Go. Call. Sloan." He grins as he exits the office.

"Man, I don't know who this new badass bitch is, but I think I love her," Lucas laughs from his seat.

I groan internally. *Not the right words to use, dumbass.*

I give Teddy a warning look. "Don't you dare, you hear me?" I tap the gun in my hand on my thigh lightly.

He bites his lip and smiles wickedly. "Whatever you say, Charlotte."

I let out a heavy loud breath. "Lucas, go sleep off the rest of the booze. I'll get you when we need you."

He opens his mouth to argue, but Carl talks before he or I have the chance. "Just do what she says, Luke. I don't want to have to call Dr. Kelly tonight because of your stupid mouth. I have no doubts she'll shoot you in your foot or something."

Lucas looks to me like he's expecting me to correct Carl, tell him I won't shoot him, but the truth is, I probably would. Nothing life-threatening, but definitely something to shut him up. I'm so sick of all of the fighting.

When all I do is raise an eyebrow at him, he laughs and stands. "Whatever you say, old man." Then he leaves the office too.

Suddenly, with almost everyone gone, I feel awkward. Teddy's eyes are on me like he's watching his prey, waiting for me to make the next move. I know he's pissed with how I've handled shit tonight, but what is he going to do? What was I supposed to do? If no one else wants to figure out something solid, then I'll be the one to do it. This is what he trained me for.

"He'll be here in less than five minutes," Julius announces when he walks back in, and I'm thankful all of the attention is off me.

"Great." I stuff my gun in the back of my jeans and pull my shirt over it before walking to the door. When I look back and see the guys just standing there, I rub my eyes. "Well, are you all coming or not? There is more to this plan than calling Cameron."

As soon as we make it to the bottom of the stairs, Sloan knocks on the door. I walk to the door and open it. "Come on in, Chief. We need to talk." I close the door as he steps inside.

"What's going on?" Uneasiness shines bright in his eyes as I turn to him.

"Everything is fine right now, but in a couple of weeks things will change."

He glances to Teddy, Carl, and Julius, then back to me. "What are you planning, Charlie?"

I give him a weak smile. I'm not sure if I just don't want to say because once I say it everything will become real, or if I really want to protect him in a way. Maybe both. "I can't tell you everything, Chief. I just need you to be on standby, and I need a little help."

The hurt that splashes onto his face is the one of a hurt father, and it doesn't surprise me. The chief has always been around, always watching, protecting, helping guide me onto the right path. But I can't risk him not agreeing. What I'm doing isn't like me, but it needs to be done.

"What kind of help?" He hooks his thumbs into his belt, then looks down.

"I need to find any information I can on the ATF agent."

He nods. "Lucky for you I've been keeping an eye on him. He's been too caught up watching you all that he hasn't thought to watch his back." He pulls a small notepad from his breast pocket and jots a few lines down. "As far as I can tell, this is where he's staying. I don't know much more than that other than his name. I can try and dig for more if you need it."

I shake my head. "Don't worry about it right now. This will

do."

I go to take the small slip of paper from him, but he doesn't let go right away. "You need to be careful, kid."

"I will." I smile.

He lets go and pulls me into a hug. "If you need anything, call me. I love you like you're my own, Charlie. Don't think I won't help you."

I close my eyes and suck in a breath. His aftershave reminds me of my dad. A spicy wintergreen smell with a sweet hint, and I revel in it. I've been so caught up with all of the shit with Teddy, I almost lost sight of what I want. I didn't come here for any other reason than to figure out my father's murder, and I'm doing just that now. I can't let him down when I've come this close so far.

He lets me go and gives me one last look before walking out the door. When he's gone, all of the guys' eyes are back on me, and Teddy is the first to speak. "Tell me the plan."

I clear the thoughts of my dad and try to tell myself I'm doing this for him. I mean, I am, but sometimes I question how much of it is for him and how much of it is for me. For the men I love.

"Emil will go down for the murders," I state flatly. "And Sloan will handle Andrew. We need to get them all at the place Emil is holding our stuff together."

"Murders?" Julius asks.

I nod. "Cameron will come, I know he will. I just pray he brings David along. I'm going to end all of this. Emil has always been a snake, I can feel it, so this is a way to get rid of him too."

"You realize what will happen if we fuck with Emil?" Carl asks from beside Teddy.

I don't need to answer his question. I do know what will happen, but I'm hoping we can find something bigger on him. Something that will turn his own people against him.

"A fucking war will ensue. Something bigger than what we're dealing with now," Teddy answers.

"I know, but you have to take risks in life. I want to go where he's keeping our supply before this goes down. He's keeping files there. It was a reckless move on his part, but I bet we can find something in there to end the war before it even begins."

"How?" Julius asks.

"Blackmail. If he doesn't cooperate, we'll take whatever we find to the feds. I won't fuck around on a small scale. This will be too big for Sloan."

"And what about his people? The ones loyal to him?" Teddy asks.

"Either we pay them off or blackmail them too. Everyone in this town has a price, and lucky for us, we have the funds."

Teddy shakes his head and steps toward me. "I don't think you've thought this through enough, Monkshood." He reaches for my face, but I slap his hand away.

"I've thought about it enough to know it'll work. And you lost the right to call me that the moment you entered my body without my consent. Don't try and use your good looks, pleading eyes, or my fucked-up love for you as a way to persuade me. I'm done waiting around for you to handle shit. We're doing this my way, and my way only. If you don't like it, go back to wherever the fuck you've been hiding out at."

All of the words flow from my mouth effortlessly. Almost too effortlessly. I've kept everything I've wanted to say to myself because sometimes I don't even know what to believe. I love Teddy, but I don't. I love Lucas, but it's wrong. I'm hurt, but I don't want to be seen as weak. Everything in my mind is so damn conflicting.

When his eyes go the slightest bit wider and his mouth opens to speak, I cut him off. "I'm done protecting everyone's feelings, Teddy. You wanted me to be like you, so here I am. Not one of you have done anything to protect my feelings or taken into consideration how I would feel about something, you just do it. Consider this as me returning the favor."

A glint of appreciation flashes over his face. "You've become so much more than I ever could have imagined."

I want to get lost in his comment. To hug him and sob into his chest because the feeling of acceptance from him makes me want to forget everything he's done. But I can't. I won't. The only thing that would do is show him it's okay that he hurt me when it isn't. Fuck all of these conflicting feelings.

I shake my head, brushing off his comment. "We need to go tonight, then we can go pay Andrew a visit. I want to make sure we have everything in place and ready before things go down."

"Emil doesn't know I'm back, so I'll stay here and keep an eye on Lucas. Take Carl and Julius with you."

"No, Carl will stay here to watch Lucas *and* you. I'll take Julius. The less bodies, the better. I don't want to draw suspicion if someone sees us."

Teddy chuckles. "Fine. Let me know what you find."

He walks away without another word as Carl follows. I watch him disappear into the kitchen before looking at Julius. "Let's handle this, Jules."

He smiles. "Can't say I agree with this plan, but I'm ready to crack some skulls, so let's do it."

CHAPTER THIRTY

Charlie

We slip into my old GTO. Everything is quiet when we pull out of the drive and start down the road. The sun is finally setting, so everything has a dusty hue to it, but in a way it's nice. Relaxing.

I shift into fourth gear when we hit the highway and try to start a conversation with Julius. I've been itching to dive deeper into everything with Lucas, and now is the perfect time to bring it up. "So, Lucas does this often?"

He looks to me, then away before throwing his long leg on the dash, stretching out as much as he can. "Not often, just when he gets too wrapped up in his own mind. One of the traits he inherited from good old dad, I guess."

I wring my hands around the steering wheel, trying to

alleviate some of the sweat building on my palms.

"You wouldn't think it, but he cares about things a lot. Sometimes too much. He takes other people's problems and makes them his own until he's to the point of madness."

"So, it was me, then?" I ask, already knowing the answer.

He flashes me a sad smile. "Everything Lucas does is on him. He's a big boy and can make his own decisions, so don't think you drove him into a bender. Were you a factor on his mind? I'm sure, but there's more to it than that."

"More to it how?"

He stares out the windshield as he talks. "When we were younger, it was always us cleaning up the messes my dad made. Taking care of mom when he beat her, lying to the cops and people at school about the bruises all over us… Basically, from the moment we were old enough to make our own decisions, Lucas deemed himself a fixer. He hasn't said it, and he probably doesn't even realize it, but his actions speak volumes.

"It doesn't matter who it is or what they've done, if Lucas feels indebted to them because they give him something, he makes it his mission to fix whatever they fuck up. My dad kept a roof over our heads somehow until…" He trails off for a moment. "He fed us, you know, all the shit a parent should do, and because of that no matter how badly he treated us, Lucas always stuck up for him in a sense. When he was finally out of the picture and Teddy took us in, he did the same thing."

I nod in understanding. "Then why do you do it?"

He looks at me with a smile. "I do it because I love my

brother. It's always going to be him and I. He's the one person I know will never leave me no matter what bad things I do. I don't always agree with him, but that doesn't matter. If he needs me, I'll be there. Love is a powerful fucking motivator."

I mull his words over in my mind, and boy is he right. After all, everything I'm doing now is because I love my dad. I haven't left the house because I know the boys need me. I love each and every one of them in different ways.

"I get that."

"I know you do, Flower. It's one of the reasons I love you too."

I give him a smile as we turn onto the road we need. Knowing Lucas has Julius makes me happy because until I work out my feelings, I think he needs that. Of course, it's said that twins share a special bond, but I think what Julius and Lucas have is more than that.

I pull into the drive and watch the overgrown grass sway in the light breeze. It doesn't look like anyone is here which makes me feel a little better about doing this. "Let's go, Jules. Whatever we can find on big clients, finances, anything—we will make it work. The bigger the better." He nods as we exit the car.

When we make it to the door of the shop, I pull the key Desi gave me from my bag and unlock it. We step inside and flip the switch by the door. Fluorescent lights buzz to life and beam down from the ceiling, illuminating everything we need to see.

I walk to the corner and check our supply, making sure everything I left is still there before I throw my bag onto a crate and start pulling open the filing cabinets closest to me.

For hours we go through numerous files containing nothing more than names, but nothing incriminating. I'm ready to give up hope—scratch my entire plan—but Julius finally finds something. "Look at this!" he exclaims, walking across the shop.

I take the file from his hands and start reading over it. Big names from our town are all over the first page, which isn't much, but when I turn to the next page, my jaw drops. Screenshots of conversations, pictures of women and young girls bloody and naked, and contracts are all neatly in order.

"This can't be right." I look to Julius and see the anger growing in his eyes.

"Well, there's no mistake. It's legit. Look at the usernames and signatures on the contracts." He points to the printed text bubbles from an online chat room, then to Emil Garcia below it, etched in perfect cursive.

"Teddy said all of his girls were willing. That he takes good care of them…" I meet his eyes again and plead with them for him to tell me this isn't true.

"You and I both know sometimes people lie and aren't who they say."

My heart sinks because I know he's talking about Teddy. I knew who Teddy was when I agreed to help him, but I didn't know the extent, I guess. I never thought he could be so terrible to me of all people—someone he swore to love.

"We have to find them, Jules. We have to get them out. I fucking knew something was up with Emil."

He nods, then takes the file back. His eyes land on a picture of a woman with blonde hair. She can't be more than my age. Her arms and legs are bound to a dirty bed, her mouth gagged with a dirty cloth. Shivers run down my spine seeing it and knowing she isn't there of her own will.

I step beside him and flip the page back to the chat room screenshots, needing something to look at other than the haunting blue eyes of the blonde woman. It's a site I've never seen, but it's clear from how they're speaking that the anonymous user is purchasing the girl.

Diablo: I promise she'll put up a good fight. She broke my man's nose when we took her, so be prepared. Payment is due upfront.

"This is disgusting," Julius whispers.

"I know. But why would he leave it here?"

Julius shakes his head. "His whole spiel of keeping important files was a bluff obviously since there isn't shit here. This one looked like it fell out of a drawer and down the back. I don't think he knows this is in here."

I nod. "Well, let's keep it that way. Don't say anything about this to anyone, you hear me? If Teddy asks, I'll handle it. I want to keep this shit quiet before we use it. I don't want Emil to see us coming."

"Okay." He nods. "But Charlie, do you know what this means?"

I grab my bag and take the file before stuffing it inside. "What?"

"This is more than a war."

We lock eyes for a moment. Thoughts race through my head, and I have no doubts they're doing the same in his head.

"I know."

CHAPTER THIRTY-ONE

Charlie

Before we got home last night, I drilled it into Julius's head to keep his mouth shut. It isn't like it's a hard request considering he barely talks anyway, but I had to voice it. I want to figure things out and try to gather more information. With what we're doing now, the only ones at stake are us. When we try and take down Emil, there are more people involved. Completely innocent people. I don't want to get them hurt in the crossfire, so a more solid plan is needed.

I push around the food on my plate. Sleep didn't come last night. My mind kept racing with every scenario possible for what we are planning, and then the faces of all of the woman and girls in the pictures wouldn't go away either. It crushes me to think they're having to experience what I went through but so much worse.

"You full?" Julius asks.

All day we've all done nothing but hang around the house. I needed to try and recoup after last night. I didn't want to go to Andrew's place right away. "No, but I'm done."

He glances to the door to make sure no one is approaching, then leans over the counter. "It's going to be okay, Flower. We'll figure it out. But I feel we should tell Teddy. He knows Emil better than us and could probably help."

"What if he already knows about it and hasn't done anything this whole time?" I ask, finally voicing the first concern that popped into my mind last night after seeing the file.

"I don't think he would stay quiet about something like that."

I level my eyes with his. "You said it yourself, sometimes people lie and aren't who we think." I throw his words back at him.

He stands back to his full height. "You're right, but there is only one way to find out. Ask him and watch his reaction. When he lies, his hands twitch by his side. He stares too intently into whoever's eyes he's talking to. I don't like him much more than you at this point, but this is bigger than just us."

"You really do just watch people, huh?"

"Someone's body language can say a lot, and it's a language that never changes." He winks. "Now, stop avoiding what I said. Ask him. I'll be right here with you."

I bite my lip. "I'm scared, Julius. I don't want to hate him anymore."

His eyes take on an understanding glint. "Queens can't be scared, Flower."

I want to let out a sarcastic laugh, but I don't. "Fine. Go get him."

He nods and walks out of the kitchen. I follow but break away at my room. I close the door behind me and lean against it, letting out a shaky breath. If Teddy is capable to do what he did to me, who's to say he would speak up for strangers?

I shake my head and push off the door. Stopping by my bed, I reach for my bag. First, I dig out my gun and tuck it into the back of my pants, then I grab the file and stuff it under my arm. When I make it back to the kitchen, Julius is already perched on a barstool next to Teddy waiting and Carl and Lucas are standing across the counter.

All of their eyes fall on me as I walk in. "We found something last night. Our smoking gun, but before we use it, I want to know if you knew."

Teddy tilts his head as Carl and Lucas step closer. "Knew what?"

I throw the file onto the counter and jut my head in its direction, telling him to open it without speaking. He picks it up with a skeptical look. He thumbs through the first couple of pages before throwing it back to the counter. Lucas picks it up and looks at the page it's opened on, then shows Carl.

"That can't be," Teddy says, standing up, raking his hands through his hair.

I glance to Julius and see him watching Teddy intently. "You know just as well as me that it's real. Did you know?"

His eyes find mine. "Of course I didn't."

I want to believe him. I don't notice any of the things Julius said he does when he's lying, but it's still hard. When someone breaks the trust you have for them, you question everything.

"I know this place though," he adds.

"What?"

"The wallpaper. I recognize it."

I look to Julius again, and he's just as surprised as me. "Well, where is it, then?"

"The basement of the casino. There are numerous rooms down there for activities. I remember seeing it when he bought the place and gave me a tour."

"He wouldn't be stupid enough to do this kind of shit there," Lucas says.

"Yeah? Well, you would think he wouldn't be stupid enough to leave something like this to be found either, huh? I'm telling you, it's the fucking casino," Teddy says with conviction.

"Well, what are we going to do, then? We can't just stand around and let it continue," Carl asks, looking to both Teddy and me.

"First," I speak before Teddy can. "We go meet with Andrew. Once we have all of this shit handled, we will deal with Emil. If all goes to plan, hopefully he'll be thrown in jail or fucking killed which will make shit easier. I don't want those girls hurt. Hell, he may not even be keeping them there for all we know. So, for now, we stick to the plan we have. We can't go in there without more information."

"So we're just going to let them suffer?" Julius finally breaks his silence.

"We have no choice right now, Julius. We have to be smart."

"Fine. Then we move things up. No waiting a couple of weeks. We do this shit tonight."

I look to Carl, Lucas, and Teddy. When none of them object, I agree. "Tonight it is, then. Let's go talk to Andrew."

We pull up to the address Sloan gave us. I was expecting something run-down or on the shadier side of town, but instead, Andrew has basically been hiding in plain sight right in the middle of town.

"You ready?" Teddy asks as the twins exit the car.

I don't know how to tell him I'm not, that I want to change my mind, but it's too late, so instead I slip my brave mask back in place. "I'm ready."

We walk into the lobby, then look at the plaques on the wall telling us which direction to go. The receptionist at the front stares at us, but I know she won't say anything. The sight of the twins covered in tattoos with their permanent "fuck off" faces doesn't leave anyone much room to want to ask questions.

We turn right and follow the hall until we reach room twelve. I wait until all of the boys are behind me before I knock. When everyone is in place, I knock hard enough to be heard, but not hard enough to startle him, then place my finger over the peephole.

The door opens a few inches, and Andrew's eye looks through the crack. "Open up, Andrew. We need to talk."

He looks to Teddy, Lucas, and Julius, then back to me. "I don't think so."

I cross my arms over my chest. "I can wait here all night, Andrew. Either open up now, or I'll find a way to get in. Not smart to get placed on the first floor." I look around him as much as I can. "Is that a window over there?" I grin.

He looks behind him, then back to me. Reluctantly, he finally unhooks the chain and opens the door.

"It's your time to shine, pig," Lucas says, plopping onto his bed.

Andrew tries to keep his eyes on all us, but he can't. He's outnumbered and he knows it which means he'll do whatever we ask.

"Everything is happening tonight," Teddy states, sitting in a chair across from the bed.

"I thought I had a couple of weeks," Andrew remarks.

I take over talking. "It's tonight or never. Are you ready or not?"

"I just have to show up and arrest the guy, right?"

I nod. "I already have the chief on board. He'll be ready to step in and help if it's needed," I lie.

"And what about Cameron?"

"Cameron won't be a problem," Teddy says, standing.

Andrew peers at each of us individually for a moment. "I can't get into anything shady. I need this to be as clean as possible."

"Worried the job won't take you back if you get tangled up in a murder?" Lucas smiles from the bed.

"How did you—"

"We know more than you think, Andrew. Just be ready for my call. If you're a minute late, I'll make sure you don't get what you need. Understand?"

He nods. "Fine. I'll be ready."

I smile and give him a piece of paper with the address on it. "Come too soon and the deal's off. Wait for my call."

"Okay." He nods again.

I can tell he's nervous. I'm nervous too, but I won't let anyone know. This web of shit has grown so much bigger than I expected. I just hope it all goes according to plan.

"We'll see you later tonight, then," Teddy says, walking to the door.

Lucas and Julius follow as he goes out the door, but I hang back for a fraction of a second to give Andrew one last warning look. "Don't fuck this up."

CHAPTER THIRTY-TWO

Charlie

"Emil?" I speak into my phone when the call connects.

"Charlotte. Is everything okay?" his thick accent coos over the line.

"No. We have a problem."

I can hear shuffling like he's moving to a quieter area before he talks again. "What kind of problem?"

"The ATF is getting closer. I got some inside info saying he found your place. I don't know how since we've been careful, but we need to move everything. Can you meet me there in a couple of hours? I'm tying up some loose ends, then I'll be there."

"Of course, of course. Call me if anything changes. I'll make the arrangements for a new spot now."

"Great." I end the call without a goodbye.

I release a breath, then send a quick text to Cameron.

Charlie: ***Come now. Hurry! We won't have a lot of time.***

I slip my phone back into my bag once I hit Send. "Cameron will be there soon, so let's hurry and get there before him." The twins and Teddy nod.

"What did Emil say?" Teddy asks.

"That he'll meet us in a couple of hours."

I bounce my knee and pick at my cuticles as I look out the window. This is really happening. I'm finally going to confront my dad's murderer. I almost want to scream with relief, but the logical side of me won't let me. I know there can be complications. I know shit can go downhill quicker than I can blink.

"Hey." Teddy grips my hand. "It's going to be okay."

I should push him away and not give him the impression I'm fine with him holding me, but I can't. Right now, something familiar is exactly what I need. A reassuring voice, a gentle touch… And Teddy knows that.

I bite my lip and squeeze his hand. "I know."

His eyes stay locked on mine for a minute before he reaches up with the other hand and tugs my lip free. I forgot how crazy the motion makes him, but he doesn't scold me or say anything about it.

He scoots closer toward me, then leans in by my ear. "I know I fucked up, Monkshood, and I know that can't be fixed, but I want you to know I do love you. I love you more than anything on this earth. I would battle the devil himself if it meant keeping you safe." He inhales a deep breath through his nose, smelling my hair. "When we go in there, stay guarded. Don't think for a single second anyone is safe until we leave, and don't let them push you around. You know what needs to be done. The boys and I will make sure nothing happens to you. Okay?"

I look back out the window, trying to hide the tears forming in my eyes. "Is that your way of saying sorry?"

When I look back to him, his blue eyes search my face. "I've never apologized for anything in my life. I don't know how to do this."

I let out a small sad laugh under my breath because I know he isn't lying. "Just say the words, Theodore."

His blue eyes battle my green ones for a moment. "I'm sorry, Charlotte."

I nod. "That's a good start."

I without a doubt believe everything he said. I know he's sorry, but he won't get away that easy. But if shit goes bad, I don't want to die knowing the man I love said sorry and I brushed it off. And a small piece of me wants to forgive him, or maybe that's the adrenaline talking.

When he looks the other way, I study his side profile. Flashbacks of the first night I saw him flood my mind followed by everything else.

Queens never let their heads fall… I've wanted you to be mine for a long time now… Because I love you, I will kill for you…

All of his words play on repeat in my mind, and it makes me realize something. Something I've refused to say or acknowledge. It isn't the murders, the guns, or the monster that is Teddy that scares me. It's the fact that I know no matter what he does, no matter what he says, I will always love him.

We pull up to the old house, but this time it feels different. When we step out, the air is thick, almost suffocating. I try to take in a deep breath, but it's like my lungs don't want to expand enough to give me what I want.

I push my bag up my shoulder, then ball my hands into fists, letting my nails dig into the soft flesh. *You can do this, Charlie*, I tell myself in my head, but it does nothing to ease my nerves.

"Are you ready?" Teddy asks, stepping beside me.

I look at Lucas and Julius at my other side, then nod. "As ready as I can be."

"Don't worry, Flower. We got you," Lucas says.

I glanced at him again. The determination in his eyes tells me he isn't lying.

In the past few months, I've gone from the chief of police's daughter to a mafia queen. I've broken out of my shell and learned more about myself than I have in years. I took enemies and made them friends, and now they're my family. I've found love and lost it, then found it again. Walking into this shop is almost bittersweet because I know at the drop of a hat, I could lose all of that.

I silence my thoughts. Now isn't the time to be mushy.

"Let's do this."

As we enter the shop, headlights flash across the window, then quickly turn off. Cameron is here. I look at the twins and Teddy. "Go wait behind the crates. If he sees you when he walks in, he'll know it's a setup. I want to hear him admit to everything before we take him down." They don't argue. One by one they disappear behind the crates of our guns.

When I hear the door open, I take one last deep breath and put on the best game face I ever will. Cameron is the first to walk in, and luckily, David is in tow.

"Cameron!" I squeal, running into his arms. "I didn't think you'd actually come." When he wraps his arms around me, I let all of the tears fall that I've been holding back. I sob into his chest.

"Hey, it's okay, Charlie. We'll get you out of this." He pets my hair.

He thinks my tears are for him, that I'm shedding them out of happiness, but that's so far from the truth. I'm weeping because I know this could be it. I can lose everything I love if I don't play this act.

I pull away from him and wipe my eyes. "Teddy will be back soon, but I have pictures and documents proving he's bad."

I reach into my bag and pull out the same file I showed him the day at the station. Only this time, I included David's picture and wrote the words "I KNOW" boldly across the front.

I should talk more, keep him under the impression I want his help, but I can't. Now that the time is here, I just want to end this. To finally get my answers.

I can see the realization hit as soon as he opens it. "You… You lied to me," he sneers.

I reach into my bag again, but he's quicker than me. He pulls the Beretta from his waist band and aims it at my face as David does the same. "You fucking lied to me!" he yells.

I close my eyes and wait after I hear the safety click off, but nothing happens. When I open them again, I see Teddy standing beside me with his gun drawn on Cameron and the twins beside him, aiming at David.

"I would think really hard about your next move, cop," Teddy roars.

Cameron looks to David, then back to Teddy but doesn't lower his gun.

"Admit it, Cameron. Tell me you killed my dad."

He shakes his head, letting his sandy hair fall over his forehead, then smiles, and it sends me over the edge. I pull my own gun out and point it at him, then walk closer, letting it rest in between his eyes. "Tell me!" I yell.

"You might as well tell the bitch, cousin," David starts from beside him. "If they don't kill us, Sebastian will. So tell her. Tell her how we made sure it was slow—how it was painful. How he scream—" David is cut off by the loud bang of a gunshot.

My ears ring and everything starts to move in slow motion. I lower my gun for a split second, only long enough to look beside me.

David's body lies on the floor with blood oozing from a

gunshot wound to his head. I would think I'd be used to it by now, seeing someone be murdered, but the shock doesn't go away and neither does the confusion. I always thought when someone is shot point-blank that their head would somehow explode and land all over the room, but that's not how it works. It's one of the many things I've learned recently.

"What have you done!" Cameron screams, looking to Teddy as he rushes to David's side.

He picks up his limp body and runs his hands all over him, almost like touching him or shaking him will make him wake up—will make this less real—but it won't.

"Admit it to her!" Teddy booms, looking down on Cameron, ignoring his soft sobs.

My body won't move no matter how much I will it to, and my mouth won't speak. I want to scream, to run away and never look back, but just like when Teddy killed Simon, nothing wants to work.

I look to the twins and see them aiming their guns at Cameron too, but I know they won't shoot. Neither will Teddy. They're respecting my demands before they kill him. "Tell her," Teddy hisses again.

Suddenly, all of the sobs and quiet pleas from Cameron fade away until they stop altogether. He stands, dropping David's dead body, then looks to Teddy. "You took away the one person I loved." He raises a shaky hand and points his gun to me. "So I'll take away what you love."

Before I can blink, another shot rings out, bouncing off all the crates and filing cabinets, then slamming back into my head. Teddy shoots at Cameron's hand, his aim almost impeccable, but when the bullet grazes, his hand jerks and his trigger is pulled.

Suddenly, a pain I've never felt in my life crashes into my body. I'm knocked down and my head bounces off the concrete floors. My vision goes hazy, but I stay awake long enough to see it. To see my entire life end.

When Teddy, Lucas, and Julius process I was shot, Teddy yells for Lucas to help me. He raises his gun again, not caring if Cameron will admit to anything now, and aims it at him. Before he can pull his trigger, his eyes lock to mine, and I mouth "I love you."

"I love—"

I don't get to hear the words. Cameron turns and fires quicker than anyone can think.

I can hear Lucas scream at Julius to get Cameron. And I can feel him touching me, trying to make sure I'm okay, but the only thing I can focus on is Teddy's body lying a few feet from mine. His blue eyes open and still locked onto me. He staring right at me, but he isn't looking at me. It's like he's looking through me. He blinks a few times, and a wave of relief and fear washes over me.

"Teddy?" I sob, but no one hears me. "Teddy!" I try louder.

"Charlie, don't move. I'm going to get help," Lucas says. His voice is shaky and high pitched.

"Help him," I get out before everything starts to turn fuzzy.

I feel Lucas leave me. I can hear hushed whispers beside

me, but eventually the static in my vision fades and everything goes black.

CHAPTER THIRTY-THREE

Teddy

I love you. I scream the words, but they won't come out. I can see her mouth moving, I think she's saying my name, but I can't be sure.

I love you. Still nothing…

Lucas leaves her and rushes to my side. I want to hit him, yell at him, something, because he should be taking care of her, not me.

"Boss?" He shakes me, dragging my eyes to his. "Hey! Don't you fucking give up on me, you hear me? We're going to get out of this."

Tears form in his eyes, and I want to comfort him, but my body won't move. Nothing wants to work.

"I…" The single word finally comes out in a weak whisper

as blood starts to choke me up and hit the back of my tongue. "I love…"

Lucas leans in closer. "You love her? I know, boss. She loves you too. That's why you gotta stick this out. You can't leave her." His hands cup my face and stare into my eyes. "You have to live, Teddy! Live for her!"

I smile because I know no matter what he says, the decision has already been made. "Take her…" I try to take a deep breath, but it's hard. I feel like an elephant is sitting on my chest. "To the beach…"

"No. No! You're going to take her, you hear me?" Lucas sobs. "You can't fucking leave us, you sorry son of a bitch!" He grabs the lapels of my suit and shakes me vigorously.

As much as I want to fight, I can't. Everything in me is gone. This is it. This is why I needed her to hate me.

I glance toward her again and try and mouth the words instead, but my mind goes blank and everything starts to fade.

As I look into her green eyes one last time as they close, I try to blink, to make sure the memory is filed into my mind, but my eyes won't open again. Everything goes black and all noise dies.

To Be Continued...

EPILOGUE

Lucas

Trying to sum up the past couple days is almost impossible. I try and replay everything in mind and make sense of what happened. It still doesn't feel real that Teddy is gone. Really gone. But when I walk through the house and he isn't there, it reminds me this is real.

I look out the window of the car and try and quiet my thoughts, but it doesn't work. It never works. But I need to be strong for Charlie. When she wakes up, she's going to have questions, and I need to be able to give her answers.

After Teddy shot Cameron, he fired an accidental shot at Charlie on his way down. Teddy was so adamant about looking at her, trying to make sure she was okay, that he never even saw Cameron level his gun with him again. A single shot to his chest took him down, and then all hell broke loose.

Julius tried to chase Cameron down when he fled, but he never could find him. We think maybe he has some sort of safe place nearby because there is no way he could have disappeared so quickly and easily. I still kick myself for that. I should have chased him and left Julius to deal with Teddy and Charlie, but I just couldn't leave them.

Sloan ended up getting Andrew though, so at least one good thing came out of this entire shit show. I still wonder if Emil has figured it out though, that we were going to set him up. When everything was said and done and Desi walked in, I didn't have the energy to question anything, and Sloan needed someone to pin things on so I could walk free. So I could take care of her.

When Carl stops in front of the hospital, I grab the bouquet of flowers and the small teddy bear I bought, then step out.

"Give me an update when you have one," he says, rolling his window down.

I nod. "Dr. Kelly said she should be waking up today. Surgery went well and there wasn't too much damage. He called her lucky…" I trail off. She's going to feel everything but lucky when she wakes up and finds out everything.

"Hey," Carl says, pulling me out of my thoughts. "Just be strong for her. She's going to be pissed and sad and probably a plethora of other things. Keep your head on for her, you hear me?"

I nod again. "I'll call when I'm done. I'm not sure how long it'll take. Go check on Julius."

"Is he still trying to get blueprints from the city?"

"Yeah. Sloan was helping him. The sooner we can figure this out, the sooner we don't have to worry. I don't want that fucking psychopath running around. Not with… Not with what's coming."

Carl nods. He knows I don't like saying the word. "I'll go check on him."

I turn and walk away as he pulls off. I go through the automatic doors, then up the elevator the same way I did the day before. When I make it to Charlie's room, I peek my head inside to see if she's up yet.

When I see she isn't, I make my way to the nurses' station. "Any updates on Welsh?" I ask.

One nurse looks at me like she's about to give the same spiel they tried on me the first day here, but when she sees my face, she closes her mouth and pulls up Charlie's chart. "Nothing yet. Dr. Kelly stopped the morphine about an hour ago. She should be waking up any second now."

"Thank you." I nod, and she blushes. Hell, she should. I don't thank anyone for shit.

When I walk through Charlie's door, I'm not surprised to see her stirring. I walk beside her bed and stand there, hoping to nip the meltdown in the bud when she wakes up.

I feel terrible I have to tell her to stay calm and keep her emotions in check when someone she loved just died, but it's for the greater good. The bigger picture.

"Lucas?" She blinks a few times, and then it happens. I see

the wheels turning as she remembers everything. "Lucas, what happened? Where's Teddy?" She starts moving frantically, trying to rip monitors off and tear out her IV.

"Charlie." I set the flowers and bear down, then place my hands on her shoulders and bring my face close to hers. "You have to stay calm."

"Calm? No! I want to see Teddy. Where is he?" She pushes me away.

"You know where he is, Charlie," I whisper, hoping she won't ask me to say it.

Tears start to fall from her lashes and coat her cheeks. "No, it was a dream. Tell me it was a dream," she begs.

"He's gone." I have to force the words out because they still hurt to even say myself.

A scream rips from her chest and bounces around the room. Her legs start to thrash, and she tries to get up.

"Charlie." I try and reason with her by grabbing her face. "Charlie!" She still blocks out everything I'm saying. "You have to stay calm! Dr. Kelly said stress isn't good for the baby!"

As soon as the word *baby* is out, her body goes still and her face goes pale…

ACKNOWLEDGEMENTS

To my husband. I love you more than words can ever express. I can't thank you enough for pushing me and believing in me. You're the best number one fan.

Teresa, Brittney, Hanna, and Krista. Thank you for being with me from the beginning. I don't think my stories would ever be as good without your feedback and love.

Sade. I love you bitch.

My cover goddess, Cat, my editor, Sandra, and my PA, Brittany. I'm so glad I found y'all! I feel I've hit the jackpot with you all. Period.

And to you, the reader. Thank you for reading my work. Thank you for supporting me. Thank you for being you! I couldn't do this without you.

FOLLOW ME!

BL lives in north Texas with her husband and three children. She enjoys writing different sub genres of romance, and building flawed and broken characters. You can most likely find her mommy-ing, watching her husband cook (because she is a horrible chef), getting tattoos, or walking into the pole you've told her to watch out for. She loves interacting with her readers and other authors in the community. Friends and family classify her as fierce, loyal and ditsy at times.

Instagram: @authorblmute

Twitter: @BlMute

Facebook: @BlMute

Facebook Group: BL's Babes

Goodreads:BL Mute

And to stay in the loop, join my newsletter!

BOOKS BY

BL Mute

The Hale Mafia Series

The Devious King

The Vengeful Queen

TSO

The Mended Universe Series

Jupiter and her Moons

Saturn and her Rings

Made in the USA
Monee, IL
29 June 2022

98822205R00138